Every Last Stitch

Doris Reidy

DEDICATION

For quilters everywhere, including my mother and sister. Their canvases are made from scraps and their brushstrokes are composed of tiny, patient stitches. With these simple tools, they create art.

ACKNOWLEDGMENTS

Thanks to Josh Langston, publisher and friend, for his inimitable cover design; to Pat Traylor for sharing her camera skills; to my fellow Verb Mongers for their critiques and encouragement; and to my children and friends, who told me they loved my first book, encouraging me to write another one.

CHAPTER ONE

2013

Grace inched her way out the back door to the patio and lowered herself gingerly into one of the Adirondack chairs. Sitting in the sunshine, listening to birdsong, always soothed her spirit. As she looked across the back yard – not as manicured as it used to be – her gaze caught and held on the wildflower garden.

Daddy loved wildflowers, she remembered, but she knew that wasn't why she cultivated her own. *I need to see them every day. I need to remember.* She found herself living in the past frequently now. Her mother, pushed to the back of her mind for years, reemerged in sharp focus.

Grace was accustomed to her load of guilt. She bore it stoically, knowing she dared not falter under its weight lest she never be able to rise again. She'd lived behind the lovely façade she'd created, and she'd been happy with her family. Why, then, did she feel such a compelling need to tell someone? Now, when it no longer mattered.

She thought about her daughters. Martha grew up exactly as Grace had hoped: strong, capable, fearless and energetic. Lavender was the child she could never have anticipated. So beautiful, but naïve and vulnerable. Always ready to take the path of least resistance because saying yes was easier than saying no. She'd protected Lavender. Tommy loved the girls, too, but he was clear-eyed about what Lavender needed.

"Let her try, and if she fails, let her deal with it," he'd said. "She needs to toughen up, learn to stand up for herself, not always depend on you or Martha to fix whatever's wrong."

"You're right, you're right," Grace would say, but somehow the next time Lavender cried over homework problems or mean girls, she'd jump right in. She couldn't help herself. And she made Martha jump in, too. She passed on fierce protectiveness as a birthright, like hair color or the shape of a chin. No telling how many messes Martha'd quietly cleaned up. No telling how many more were to come. Grace knew she'd failed both her girls in an essential way.

It had been two years since Tommy's death. Sometimes she felt that he'd just stepped out and would be back any minute. Other times, she could barely remember his face. How strange that they were both destined to die so young, barely in their sixties. He'd loved her with a devotion so bright it illuminated her life. She couldn't have chanced losing it. No, she'd been wise to keep her secret. It was too late for second thoughts. Yet, the desire to unburden herself was so strong it couldn't be denied.

She rose painfully and made her way back through the house to her bedroom. Sitting at her little desk, she took a sheet of paper and a pen and wrote, "It was monkshood. I had to finish it, and I'm not sorry. I wish it could have been different." Bending dizzily, she pulled a flat box from beneath the bed, opened it, put the paper inside, and shoved it back under the bed with her foot.

There. The girls would find it someday and not know what to make of it, but somehow she felt better. Exhausted, she lay back on the pillows and pulled up the soft throw that lay across the bed.

So tired. I'll have a little rest. Not sleep. Just close my eyes. Tommy. I was just thinking about you. I've been wanting to tell you something. You always knew? My love..."

CHAPTER TWO

2014

"For heaven's sake, Lavender, be careful," Martha said, not for the first time.

The sisters trod carefully, checking their hair for spiders. The attic was a place of slanted light where dust motes danced. Cobwebs draped the rafters and dipped low to set traps for unwary heads. One careless step could plunge a leg through the floor, destroying the ceiling of the room below. Their destination, a row of storage boxes and an old trunk, squatted on a random piece of plywood under the dormer window.

Lavender had a tendency to daydream, even in hazardous circumstances. She was alert to the possibility of spiders, though. Martha watched with a mixture of amusement and exasperation as Lavender ran her fingers cautiously through her mane of blue-black hair. She wondered again how someone so beautiful could be so adrift in the world.

Martha had never been adrift. She knew her place:

with her husband, and their two teenage boys, both of whom would eventually be going off to college, making suitable marriages, and producing adorable grandchildren, in that order. That was reality. Reality was where Martha felt most comfortable and where she made sure to stick tight. She could not have been more different than her sister.

Lavender's fancy and fanciful name came when their otherwise-practical mother, Grace, gazed for the first time into her baby girl's eyes, so dark blue they looked purple.

"That color may not last," the pediatrician warned. "Her eyes may change color completely by the time she's nine months old."

But Grace had seen eyes like that before and she knew better. *It will be different this time, different for this child*, she vowed silently. And somehow, over the years, those violet eyes exempted Lavender from the mundane aspects of living. Like the lilies of the field, she toiled not, neither did she spin.

All her life, Martha'd heard the story of how she got her name. She was named after Martha in the Bible story, the one who cooked and cleaned while her sister, Mary, sat at Jesus' feet. It had been their mother's intention, until she looked into those remarkable eyes, to name the new baby Mary to complete the Biblical allusion. So, added to natural sibling jealousy was the knowledge that Lavender was set apart, special, right from the start.

At the age of eight, Martha heard the word "lavatory" for the first time at school, and immediately latched onto the shortened version, "lav," as a nickname for her little sister. It seemed the height of cleverness.

"Lav, Lav, pee-pot Lav," she'd chanted, some dark part of herself glad to see Lavender's eyes brim with tears.

Martha hadn't expected and couldn't forget the way

her mother had grabbed her arm and yanked her to the kitchen sink. She'd scoured her daughter's mouth with soap, whacked her bottom, and hissed, "Never, *never* talk like that to your sister again!"

Then Martha watched, wide-eyed, as her mother cried and went to bed with a migraine. She knew she'd done something unforgiveable, something she must never do again. Years later, hearing Shakespeare's line, "What's in a name?" she thought she could have told him: plenty.

Martha gave herself a mental shake and focused. Since their mother's death, Martha and Lavender had remained in their childhood home, sorting and organizing the possessions of a lifetime. Today's mission was clearing out the attic. Grace and Tommy McGuire had lived in this house their entire married lives. After Tommy's death two years earlier, Grace dug in her heels, deaf to Martha's praise of a nearby retirement community.

"This is my home," she'd said, "and I want to stay here until I die." Which she did. Nobody expected the time she had left to be so brief. After her death, it fell to her daughters to decide what to do with years of accumulated stuff, a task made worse by the sisters' disagreements. Martha was anxious to pull everything out of closets, drawers and boxes, sort through it, make piles to discard, donate or keep, then clean up and clear out. She was anxious to get back to her house, her family and her life. She was anxious about most everything. It went with the territory of being the responsible one.

Lavender, on the other hand, wanted to keep her childhood home intact for a while longer. She wanted to sleep in her mother's bed wearing one of her nightgowns, make meals from her mother's recipe books and eat them off the familiar plates. Martha caught her crying over blackened old cookie sheets used in their childhood, reminiscing about chocolate chip cookies. Nothing, apparently, was too trivial to escape her sentimental regard. Lavender annoyed her sister intensely by referring to the house as "our home place."

"It's just an empty house!" Martha said emphatically. "We need to get it on the market this summer to take advantage of buyers who want to get settled before school starts. And as for the furniture and other stuff, once the people who lived in a house are gone, their possessions qualify as junk to anyone who doesn't have a sentimental attachment."

"But I do," Lavender said, "I do have a sentimental attachment."

And she drifted from room to room, running her hand over the patina of an old table, pleating the curtains between her fingers. Martha sent her to sort books and found her hours later deep into *Little Women,* in tears over Beth's death. Asked to sweep the basement, Lavender instead wandered down memory lane at her father's workbench.

"Remember when Daddy tried to fix the leak in the bathtub faucet and there was a geyser of water that hit the ceiling?" she asked, when Martha came to see why no sweeping was being done. "Here's the wrench he was using. Remember how he cussed and threw it across the room, and it chipped the tile and that made him even madder. We all laughed so hard he finally had to laugh, too."

Their father had loved to invent unusual features for the old house, and he had enough handyman skills to tackle anything. Instead of conventional pull-down stairs to the attic, for example, he'd made a series of bookshelves that stepped up the wall of the wide central hallway to the twelve-foot ceiling. There was no handrail, and the tops of the shelves that served as stairs were narrow, slippery and treacherous. That had been a welcome-home present when

Grace returned from the hospital with Lavender in her arms. Years later, Grace admitted to her grown daughters that she'd wept with frustration at the prospect of keeping two lively youngsters off those dangerous stairs.

Then there was the broom closet shoe-horned into a twelve-inch space beside the refrigerator; when you opened the door, shelves rolled out on wheels. A pulley hoisted laundry up to the basement ceiling for use on rainy days before they could afford a clothes dryer. The doorbell button was wired to automatically turn on the porch light when pushed. The house was full of cubbies, niches, and storage spaces hidden behind panels. The girls' friends had loved to come over and play hide and seek.

The sisters laughed as they reminisced about their father's constant tinkering, until Martha said, "Okay, enough of that. Come on, let's just get this done."

The week they'd allotted was almost up, and they'd worked their way up to the attic. *Well, I worked our way up*, Martha thought. *If it was up to Lavender, we'd still be sitting around drinking Earl Grey tea out of Mom's tea cups, or banging our thumbs with one of Dad's hammers, just for the nostalgia of it.*

There was a row of big, black trash bags at the curb, ready for pick up on garbage day, and another row in the garage to be given to the next charity that called for donations. The contents of the kitchen cabinets were untouched, however, and their mother's clothing still hung in her closet. Her eyeglasses lay neatly folded on her library book. *I must return that book*, Martha thought. Efforts to engage Lavender in disposing of such intensely personal items had been unsuccessful because they ended in tears. So Martha suggested they tackle the attic. It had to be done sooner or later, and maybe it wouldn't be such a minefield of work-stopping memories.

The attic hadn't been used much by their parents. There was no floor except for a few sheets of plywood laid over the rafters, and access was limited by the perilous climb up the bookcase steps, a trip her mother had long ago stopped making. The contents had been undisturbed for years. Martha opened the first plastic storage box to find mementos from their school days: report cards, class photographs, awards. Martha got a perfect attendance certificate; Lavender received a slender volume of *Leaves of Grass* as a prize for some long-forgotten poem.

When she saw it, she cried, "Oh! *Leaves of Grass!* I love Walt Whitman," and plunked down on the plywood to read it again, right then and there.

Martha gave up on getting her sister to help, left her to Walt Whitman, and opened the next storage box. It was full of old magazines with dog-eared pages, testimonies to project ideas that never took root, and newspaper clippings of long-forgotten provenance. She wrote TRASH on a Post-It note, stuck it to the top of the box, and moved on. After sighing her way impatiently through three more boxes containing various items of dubious or no value, she came at last to the old trunk. She could remember seeing that trunk in her earliest memories, squatting in one corner or another like a big, black toad. Occasionally, her mother would deposit something in it, never failing to vow that someday she would pull everything out and organize it. It hadn't happened then, but it was going to happen now. Martha gingerly lifted the lid.

The top layers were fraying hand-made Afghans deemed by her mother too precious to throw away, but not good enough to use. Martha promptly placed them in the discard pile. Then a stratum of mysterious scraps of fabric surfaced, all sizes and colors. She recognized patterns from a couple of her old school dresses and some floral sheets, but couldn't imagine why her mother had saved them. Into the discard pile they went.

On the very bottom of the trunk, sheathed in blue tissue paper, she found squares of fabric yellowed with age. Martha unwrapped the top ones and saw that they were printed with letters of the alphabet, each one elaborately decorated. The letter A was entwined with apple blossoms; B was nearly hidden in honeysuckle vines abuzz with tiny bees; C stood tall in a bed of catnip, complete with a miniscule gray kitten.

Charmed, Martha unwrapped all the blocks and laid them out in order. She saw that they were meant to be embroidered and then pieced together for a quilt, probably for a crib. Judging from the yellowed fabric, it looked like most of them had been completed by long-dead hands, but the letter R, in a tangle of climbing roses, had only been started. There were rusty stains on that square and a threaded needle still stuck into it, as though someone had laid it aside for a moment, meaning to pick it up again soon. The remaining squares, S through Z, were unstitched.

"Lavender, look at this," Martha said.

"Hmmm?" Lavender looked up dreamily from her book. "What did you find? Money, I hope. Big piles of thousand-dollar bills."

"Not money, but come and look at these quilt blocks. There's no telling how old they are. Have you seen them before? I haven't."

Lavender thumbed through the blocks. "They're darling. No, Mom never showed me these. I don't remember her ever doing needle work."

"She didn't. She said she had three left thumbs and hated anything that took fine motor coordination. Remember how we used to wish she'd sew our Halloween costumes like the other mothers did, instead of getting us those cheap things from the store?"

"I do," Lavender said with a smile. "I remember one year all I wanted was to be a ballerina, and I begged and begged her, 'make me a tutu, make me a tutu.' Finally, she waved her wooden spoon at me and said, 'Presto Chango, you're a tutu.'"

The sisters' laughter erased their differences for the moment. *There will always be this bond of shared memories,* Martha reflected, *no matter how annoyed I get or how vague Lavender becomes.*

"Wouldn't it be nice," Lavender said, "wouldn't it be the neatest thing if you and I finished these blocks, and made them into a quilt? Maybe for your first grandchild. Think of the history."

"Do you know how to embroider? And quilt? Because I sure don't."

"Not really, no. But this is cross stitch. It's pretty basic, see, just making an x over and over on the pattern. I think I remember Aunt Pat teaching us to cross stitch, but I've never quilted, or even watched anyone quilt."

"Well, how do you propose we'd finish this quilt, then?"

"We could learn," Lavender said, "and think what a wonderful tribute a finished quilt like this would be to all the women in our family who must have worked on it through the years. I wish we'd known them, but we can sort of know them by finishing what they began."

"It's a sweet idea, but when would we have time? I've got to get back to Zach and the kids. They're probably about ready to start eating each other by now. Nobody but me seems to know how to cook."

"Sure, I know; your family needs you. You have lots of responsibilities."

Martha looked at Lavender sharply but saw no signs of sarcasm in her face.

"But I could stay on for a while," Lavender continued. "I'd like to, really. My apartment is still sub-let for another six months, and—well, I moved out of Kevin's place."

"You did? You never said a word about it."

"It just got a little fraught. He had...different ideas about things."

"Like what?"

"Oh, you know, 'I am your lord and m-master, you will obey me.'"

"Yikes. He needs to get over that attitude before he's husband material."

"I won't be marrying Kevin, you can count on that," Lavender said. "I don't like to b-be...I don't like to be b-bullied." The old childhood stutter, long overcome, still surfaced in times of stress.

"Was he mean to you? Did he hurt you?" Martha asked in horror. Of all Lavender's many breakups, none had ever ended on bad terms. Often, ex-suitors hung around an embarrassingly long time in hopes of reconciliation, but eventually they all went peacefully.

"Oh, just forget it. Really, it's over," Lavender answered with a vague little wave of her hand.

Martha knew she'd get no more out of her sister today, but she promised herself she'd be on the lookout for Kevin. And he'd better hope she didn't see him.

CHAPTER THREE

1962

Grace bent her head over the quilt square in her lap, trying not to shed the tears that filled her eyes. Mother would not be happy if she wet it with what she called Grace's sniveling. It was a perfect Saturday morning, and the sun was beckoning her to come outside. She could hear her friends chanting a tantalizing jump-rope rhyme.

Her best friend, Janice, knocked bravely on the door and Grace heard her say, "Please, Miz Strunk, can Grace come out?" She couldn't hear Mother's reply, but Grace knew very well there would be no outdoor time until the quilt block was finished.

Resignedly, she jabbed her embroidery needle into the fabric, only to puncture one of her fingers. In horror, she watched the red blood stain blossom on the letter R she was embroidering. The R was entwined with vines and roses, and for a wild moment she hoped maybe Mother would think the blood was a rose.

Whack!

The metal ruler cut across her hand, leaving an oozing red welt. Mother stood over her with the ruler raised to strike again. Her unusual eyes, eyes that looked purple in some light, shot forth sparks of fury.

"Do you see what you've done?" Mother said. When she was really angry, she spoke in a hissing whisper. Grace would have preferred yelling.

"These quilt squares were handed down to me from my family, and now you've ruined one."

The ruler descended again and again, until Grace's hands were a cross stitched sampler of welts leaking tiny beads of crimson. She knew better than to cry out or try to avoid the blows. Nothing made Mother madder. Grace forced herself to concentrate on a baby rabbit she'd seen once, sitting absolutely immobile as it waited for its mother to return. *Be that still, be that still,* she repeated to herself.

Eventually, Mother got tired. Throwing the ruler down, she slammed out of the room. Grace got up quietly and went into the bathroom, where she applied stinging iodine to the cuts and plastered the backs of her hands with Band-Aids. Mother didn't care how many Band-Aids she used, a rare departure from the frugality that ruled the house. She supposed wearily that Mother preferred not to see the results of her temper once her anger was spent. Or maybe she didn't want anyone else to see.

Grace took her time pressing a cold washcloth to her eyes to eliminate any traces of tears. Mother simply hated what she called a po'-faced child, and Grace couldn't risk setting her off again. But when she finally emerged from the bathroom, she was greeted by the delectable aroma of peanut butter cookies baking in the oven. All signs of the alphabet quilt square, embroidery thread and scissors were swept away. Mother was humming in the kitchen.

"Come here, Grace," she called.

Mother slid the first batch of hot cookies out of the oven and put some on a plate. She poured two glasses of milk and motioned for Grace to join her at the table.

"Time for a little treat," Mother said. "Come on, honey."

This baking mother bore no resemblance to the hissing, hitting mother, something Grace always found totally confusing. How could she switch moods so quickly and so completely? Grace knew she'd feel shaky and wary for the rest of the day as a result of the punishment she'd just endured, but Mother seemed to have forgotten all about it. Swallowing the cookie was hard when her throat was so dry, but Grace managed, and then thanked Mother politely. Just as if nothing was wrong.

"Run on out and play now," Mother said, brushing up the cookie crumbs and rinsing the glasses. "Come back in time for dinner."

Grace escaped out into the bright day, but she no longer wanted to join her friends with the jump rope. Questions about her hands would be sure to follow, and she needed time to think of a convincing lie. It was important, vitally important, that she never tell anyone what went on in her home. Mother said Grace could become a foster child if she told. Unsure what a foster child was, Grace nevertheless knew she didn't want to be one, so she was ready when asked by a friend or a friend's mother, "What happened?"

"I fell against the door and cut my lip; I burned my leg on the oven door; I stumbled in the dark." She was always prepared. It had been impossible, however, to explain the bald patch that resulted when Mother grabbed a handful of hair, and lifted her from the floor. She'd had to do a comb-over that looked so odd it raised comments of its own. Only Janice knew the real reason for the bruises and she had promised pinkie-swear that she would tell no one. Peering through the branches of the tree in which she'd taken refuge, Grace saw her coming now. Janice was a sturdy little girl in pigtails, often sporting skinned knees. She had a nice mother and dad, a pesty little brother, a canopy bed, and a real diary with a tiny lock and key. Grace couldn't help being envious.

"Janice! Up here," she called softly.

Janice scrambled up to join her on their favorite branch in the old cherry tree. The limbs were perfectly spaced for climbing, the leaves were thick enough to hide them, and when the cherries were ripe the girls raced the birds to see who could eat the most. Grace cherished this hiding place because Mother never thought to look up when she was hunting her. It was only good during the summer, though.

"Oh, Grace, your poor hands," Janice said, catching sight of Grace's many Band-Aids. "What happened? Do you want my Mom to bandage them for you?"

"No, I don't want your Mom to know. Mother hit me with a ruler because I stuck myself with a needle and got blood on a quilt square. I put iodine on the cuts."

" Gosh, did you cry a lot?"

"It's better if I don't. Then it's over sooner. She said if I ever told, I might have to be a foster child."

Janice nodded doubtfully, impressed by Grace's solemn tone. Strange were the ways of grown-ups, both girls knew that, and like little animals they accepted whatever came their way.

"Aren't you scared of her?" Janice asked Grace. It wasn't necessary to define "her."

"I am, sometimes," Grace said. "Her eyes look really mean when she loses her temper. I try to stay out of her way when she acts like she's getting mad, but lots of times I'm not quick enough. It's been worse since Daddy died. He used to make her stop. She acts nice after she gets over being mad, though."

"I brought you something," Janice said. Reaching into the pocket of her dress, she brought out a diary just like her own. The little key was taped to the shiny gold lock, promising privacy for whatever was written within. Grace caught her breath.

"Janice! It's beautiful," she said.

"It's for your birthday," Janice said simply.

"Oh. I forgot. Mother didn't say anything about my birthday."

"Don't let her know you have it," Janice cautioned. "She'd take it away, for sure."

"I'll hide it; I know just the place," Grace said. "Thank you so much." She hugged Janice awkwardly amid the tree branches. "I'll write in it every day. Should I wait until January first to start?"

"You can start any time, even in the middle of summer," Janice said.

"I'll just write my name inside the cover," Grace decided. She wanted to savor the anticipation of writing the first lines in the pristine little book. Pleasure deferred was pleasure unspoiled by the violence of her day-to-day life.

"I can't wait until I grow up," she said, "and then I'll leave this house the minute I can, and never see Mother again."

"That will take a long time," Janice said, thinking of the interminable stretch just between breakfast and dinner.

"I know. But what else can I do?"

~*~

Mother's temper did not improve as Grace reached adolescence. Each manifestation of normal growth—her first bra, shaving her legs, a crush on a classmate—had to be cloaked in deepest secrecy. But Mother always found out anyway. She noticed the outline of the bra beneath the blouse and demanded, between blows, to know where Grace had gotten it. (Janice, of course, but Grace wouldn't say, no matter how much Mother hit her.) The tell-tale stubble on Grace's legs brought forth Mother's leather belt, and she criss-crossed those legs with welts. When she found the crumpled notebook page in the wastebasket on which Grace had scribbled Mrs. Tommy McGuire, Grace McGuire, over and over, she made Grace eat an entire bar of soap, bringing on violent vomiting that lasted for hours.

Mother had gotten craftier. She tried to leave bruises only in places that didn't show. Purple pinch marks on Grace's arms could be hidden under long sleeves, welts on her legs under jeans. If Mother slipped up and created a black eye or a fat lip, it could always be explained away by Grace's long-documented history of clumsiness.

"I don't know how that child manages to bang herself up so," Mother said to a neighbor over the back fence.

The neighbor looked skeptical, but said nothing. Grace's treatment was not the dark secret that both she and her Mother imagined. But people minded their own business.

~*~

Seventh grade health class was a pivotal rite of passage in the middle school Grace attended. Everyone knew that health class was actually about sex, a daring idea for public education in their little town in the 1960s. The children were separated by gender so they could speak freely.

The girls were taught by a woman named Mrs. Winechester. A large, gregarious woman given to wearing colorful, large prints and flowing scarves, she loved teaching because of the opportunity it gave her to monologue without interruption. Textbooks remained unopened while she talked during the entire class period, spilling a cornucopia of information before her bedazzled captive audience. Most of the girls had recently experienced their first menstrual periods and were newly interested in boys. In this class, the most embarrassing questions could be asked and answered in a non-judgmental atmosphere. The girls presented Mrs. Winechester with a sea of upturned, rapt faces, alight with the conviction that this was one adult who really understood them.

It was in health class that Grace first thought maybe—just maybe—she could talk to this teacher about what went on at home.

Mother had been especially horrible that year. The cookie-baking days were long forgotten. Grace missed those little islands of serenity when Mother seemed not only to tolerate her, but even to like her a little bit. Mother smoldered angrily all the time now, with sudden, unpredictable bouts of fury. Grace never knew what would bring them on, and her best efforts not to provoke Mother were unsuccessful.

For instance, when her period started and she asked for sanitary supplies, Mother had flown into a rage and slugged her in the face with a closed fist that triggered a copious nosebleed, and, quite possibly, a broken nose. Dr. Flanagan was not consulted.

"You mealy-mouthed little brat!" Mother screamed. "I guess this means you'll be getting yourself pregnant now. Well, I'll fix you so no boy will look at you."

"Please, Mother, I'm sorry, I can't help it. Please, stop

hitting. If you'll just give me some money, I'll walk to the store and get what I need."

"Oh, yes, give you money! It will be a pretty day when I give you money to walk anywhere. You can figure out how to deal with the curse as best you can. You deserve every bit of it."

So Grace went to Janice, tears and blood mingled on her face.

"Please, Janice, can you let me have some pads? Mother won't..." she gulped, unable to continue.

"Oh, golly, your face! Let me get Mom."

"No, no, please don't get your Mom. I'll be all right. I just need—you know."

"Of course. Here, take these. Mom will get me some more. Grace, are you sure you shouldn't tell somebody about the way your mother hits you? It seems to be getting worse. I'm scared for you."

"I've been thinking I might tell Mrs. Winechester. Do you think I should?"

"Yes, definitely. She'll know what to do."

But Mrs. Winechester didn't, although she wasn't completely ignorant of Grace's situation. She'd heard talk in the teachers' lounge. One of the new hires, Miss Petrelli, was full of ideals and reformer's zeal. She was especially upset when she saw Grace's bruises, revealed by a sleeve accidentally pushed up or a collar turned down.

"We have to do something to help Grace Strunk," Miss Petrelli said. "She is obviously being abused. Has anyone notified the principal? Or tried to talk to the mother?"

Mrs. Winechester took Miss Petrelli aside. "Now, dear, think about it. What if you brought an accusation that proved to be false? Thirteen-year-old girls are not the most reliable sources. No sense in courting trouble with the principal and the police, and maybe even the school board. You're new here; this is your first year of teaching. You don't want to stir up a hornet's nest that might become part of your employment history. Better just do your job at school and let parents handle things at home. That's how we all feel."

Miss Petrelli was silenced.

So Mrs. Winechester had given it some thought and was prepared when Grace came to her after school one day. She listened to Grace's halting recital of abuse, then chose her words carefully.

"Grace, I'll tell you confidentially that my mother and I had terrible fights when I was your age. I just downright hated her when I was thirteen. It seemed she lived to make my life miserable. It's difficult sometimes for mothers to accept that their little girls are growing up, and daughters— well, we girls can be dramatic, can't we?"

She winked at Grace conspiritorily, pausing to allow her to speak.

"I know, but it's not like that, Mrs. Winechester. My mother gets—it's like she goes crazy. It's worse lately. I think she might kill me."

"Now, see, Grace, that's exactly what I mean about drama. I'm sure your mother loves you very much, and she is certainly not going to kill you. What an idea! I want you to try something: be an extra-good girl for one month. Be sweet to your mother, no sassing, do everything she tells you, and help more around the house. Then come back to me at the end of the month, and I bet you'll tell me things are much better at home."

Grace looked at the floor, her eyes burning with tears

she'd learned not to shed. If only the solution to her problems were that simple. This teacher would be no help. She was on her own, just as she'd always been. It was up to her to figure out how to handle Mother.

CHAPTER FOUR

2014

Looking back, Martha wasn't sure when it happened, but somehow Lavender was firmly ensconced in their mother's house. The original plan was to spend a week cleaning and clearing, and at the end of that week Martha went back to her home and family. What good were plans if you didn't stick to them? Lavender stayed on "temporarily." The days turned into weeks. Stopping by one day, Martha found her wearing a pair of their mother's baggy elastic-waist shorts, bent over to weed a flower bed. For a disorienting moment, Martha thought her mother had returned from the dead.

"Lavender, look at yourself. How old did you say you were, again? Seventy?"

"Oh, hi, Martha. I know, I know, I look awful, but there's nobody here to see me. And these shorts rock. No binding or pinching. I might have to start shopping in the silver-hair section myself."

"Well, you've got the yard looking nice, anyway. The hydrangeas are gorgeous this year, and the wildflower garden is beautiful. Mom would be proud, she loved those plants. How are you coming on the inside of the house?"

"Mmmmm. Not so good. I actually haven't made much progress."

"Much?"

"Any."

"We've got to get the house ready to sell; we agreed to put it on the market this summer. You know that. What is your problem?"

"I just hate to sell our home place to strangers. And I like it here. I don't see why I can't just stay indefinitely."

"One big reason is that everything Mom had was left to us equally. If you take possession of the biggest asset, the house, where does that leave me?" Sometimes you had to hit Lavender over the head with reality.

"Oh. I never thought of it that way. You're right. I should buy your share if I want to stay here."

"And that's not going to happen, is it?"

"Well, you never know," Lavender said vaguely.

But Martha knew that Lavender never had money unless she was with a well-heeled man. At present, there didn't seem to be any men at all in the picture, well-heeled or not; ergo, no money. Her sister managed to live without holding a steady job. She had a small income from sub-letting her apartment, but it was just spending money, really. Sometimes she'd take a temporary position: holiday retail, pet sitter, telephone sales. Nothing lasted long, and the little bit of money she made didn't last long, either. Then Martha's husband would have to write a check to Lavender's landlord or dentist or bank, and his resigned sigh always filled Martha with guilt by association. It didn't seem to bother Lavender, however, who always accepted gratefully and then promptly forgot about repayment. Martha's gloomy train of thought was derailed by Lavender's question.

"Martha, did Mom ever tell you anything about her childhood?"

"No, she never talked about it. I always thought it was odd that we knew nothing about her side of the family. All she ever said was that she was the only child of two only children, and that both her parents were dead. I got the feeling that the subject was off-limits. If I ever mentioned it, Mom got all stiff and funny-acting, so I learned not to go there."

"Well, I found something I can't understand. There was a box of papers under Mom's bed - one of those fire-proof boxes - and it contained another copy of her will, the deed to the house, car title, stuff like that. There's this one sheet of paper that looks recent. It's in Mom's handwriting, but shaky, like her writing was at the end. Here, I'll show you."

Lavender fished in the pocket of her baggy shorts and pulled out a crisp, folded sheet of paper. She opened it and read, "'It was monkshood. I had to finish it, and I'm not sorry. But I wish it could have been different.'"

"Sorry about what? And what's monkshead?"

"Monks*hood,* and it's a plant. Mom has always grown it. See, there it is in the wildflower garden. That tall, blue one in the middle, the one we were forbidden to touch."

"Okay, I remember that. But...she's not sorry for growing a wildflower? What does that mean?"

The sisters looked at each in bewilderment. Their mother had been the least mysterious creature imaginable, except for her reticence about her family of origin. This cryptic note didn't sound like her at all.

Lavender thought for a minute. "Do you think Aunt Pat could tell us anything?"

"She's Dad's sister, so she probably didn't know much about Mom until Dad married her. But they all grew up in the same small town, so maybe she's heard things over the years. It wouldn't hurt to ask."

"I want to talk to her about finishing that quilt, anyway," Lavender said. "Let's call her and see if she has time to see us."

"Right now?"

"Sure, why not? Better yet, let's just drop in."

~*~

Pat McGuire was surprised to see both her nieces appear unannounced on her doorstep on a run-of-the-mill Tuesday morning.

"What's wrong?" she demanded, alarmed. "Did somebody die? Wait, everybody but me is already dead."

Martha and Lavender assured her their visit was not a death announcement. Then, amid many exclamations of relief and invitations to "Come in, come in, girls!" they were ushered into Pat's sitting room. Always referred to as the "front room," it was where she took her infrequent guests. Indeed, it was the only room in the house with room for guests. Pat was, if not a hoarder, a pack-rat of the first order. Her home was filled, literally filled, with the detritus of many years of collecting and scavenging. Ask her what use she could possibly have for this or that odd object and she'd say, "Well, I'm planning to paint it (or decoupage it, or strip it), and then it will be worth some money." If all the items Pat thought worth some money were actually exchanged for cash, she'd be a wealthy woman. But she couldn't bear to part with her treasures, so they accumulated, piling up in drifts in the bedrooms, the sun porch, hall and stairway, in the garage and attic, spilling into the backyard to the disquiet of her neighbors, and finally even invading the sacrosanct corners of the front room.

As a former Army nurse, Pat said she'd had enough rules and regulations to last her a lifetime. "I'm never living out of a suitcase again," she said. "Nobody will ever be allowed to inspect my quarters, so I'm having things just the way I want them."

Martha developed tics and twitches after a few moments in Pat's house. Her fingers itched to start sorting and discarding and she had to fold her hands to keep them still. She'd offered many times to help her aunt "get organized," as she tactfully put it, but Pat always declined with thanks. She'd get to it one of these days, she said, and meanwhile, she didn't want anyone else discarding items that were, well, worth some money.

Lavender seemed unaware and unmoved by the chaos around her. She settled into the only open corner of the sofa and accepted a cup of tea.

"You know we're cleaning out Mom's house," she began. "It makes us realize that we actually know so little about her background. She never talked about her side of the family. We wondered if you could tell us more."

Pat looked thoughtful. "Grace was a dark horse, I always said. Kept herself to herself. Of course we all went to the same elementary school, although she and Tommy were four years behind me. It was a mighty small town, but Grace and her mother didn't socialize at all. We were surprised when Tommy started going out with her. When they got serious, he brought her home. Mama did her usual third-degree, but Grace was so vague Mama couldn't get anything out of her. She warned your Dad, she said, 'Son, a woman without family has got to have something wrong with her.' Not that our family was any great shakes, what with Dad's drinking and all. But Tommy was in love, he didn't care, he said he'd marry her no matter what, which he did. And I think they were happy together. All those years, and having you girls, and then the grandchildren came along—yes, I think your folks were happy."

Martha swam into this flow of words with another question. "Well, one thing we do know is that Mom loved to garden. Did she ever say if she learned about plants from her mother?"

"She said once that she liked to read about botany. I asked her if she studied it in college, but she got all vague like she could do, and then somehow we were talking about something else, and botany was never mentioned again."

"Did she talk about her home life, her mother?" Lavender asked.

"No." Pat was definite. "And I asked her a time or two. She'd just start in on a different topic and never would answer. But I found out some things in a round-about way."

Pat hesitated; then she made up her mind to speak. "I don't like to gossip about the departed, but I might as well tell you. No harm now. Once I ran into an old friend of your Mom's at a genealogy meeting. Remember that group I used to go to when I was researching our family tree? There was a woman there—I recall her name was Janice—and we got to talking about where we were from and ancestors and all that, and it turned out she was from our home town. I kind of remembered her when I thought hard about it, but she was younger than me, so our paths didn't cross. She was the same age as Grace, and I asked if she knew her. Well, they were childhood best friends, Janice and Grace. Her face just lit up when I said Grace was my sister-in-law. But then she looked sad, and said Grace had a really hard time of it growing up. I asked why, and she said, 'Her mother,' and then she clammed up. I got the feeling she didn't want to talk about it and I didn't press her. I never mentioned it to Grace; I just had a feeling the subject was taboo."

"We always had the same feeling. Mom never talked about her mother, except to say that she was dead," Martha said, "so I guess she wanted to leave the past in the past. We should respect that, Lavender."

"She was a good mother to us, no matter what she had to overcome. It's hard to see your parents objectively and think that they had a whole life you knew nothing about," Lavender said.

They pondered this truth in silence for a few minutes. Then Lavender said, "One of the things that made us think about Mom's childhood was these quilt blocks that we found in the attic. They appear to be old, like they've been saved for years, and we wondered about their origin. Look, I've brought them." Lavender pulled the blocks from her tote bag and laid them out on the only uncluttered area of the carpet.

Pat leaned over to look. "Why, yes, I've seen patterns like these before," she said. "People used to make such quilts for baby gifts. Sweet, aren't they?"

"Did you ever see Mom working on them?"

"No, can't say that I did. Your Mom didn't do needlework."

"Would you show us how to finish the blocks and make a quilt?" Lavender asked. "I think it would be a great way to reconnect with the past, even though we'll never know the women who worked on the blocks before us."

"Why sure, honey, I'd love to. What a great idea."

35

Pat's white head and Lavender's dark one bent over the blocks as they planned future quilting bees. Martha heard "next Tuesday," and "what supplies should I get?" and saw significant glances being sent her way. Sensing she was about to be roped into organizing the whole thing, she knew exactly how to bring the visit to a speedy end.

"Aunt Pat," she said, "why don't I come over one day next week, and help you tackle some of this stuff. We could sort it all into piles..."

But Pat was on her feet. "My, look at the time," she said. "Why, girls, I nearly forgot I've got a, uh, a doctor appointment this morning. I hate to rush you out, but I've got to get ready."

Talking non-stop, she shooed her nieces before her like two chickens, sweeping them out the front door and down the walk to their car without pausing for breath. Before they knew it, they were on their way in a flurry of waves and "You girls come back, now."

Lavender was quiet on the way home. When they reached the familiar old driveway, she paused before getting out of Martha's car.

"Poor Mom," she said. "I wonder what her childhood was like. I wish we could ask her. She might have told us if we'd asked. Now we'll never know."

"If it was anything really bad," Martha said, "something we needed to know, don't you think Dad would have told us?"

CHAPTER FIVE

1970

Grace stroked the long black gown that hung on the hook on her closet door. The companion mortarboard lay on the dresser. At last - at *last* - she'd be graduating from high school. Final exams had been taken and passed. Her grades were excellent, and all the necessary credits were lined up in neat rows on her transcript, credits that would march her off to college. She would escape this house and her mother. She would escape alive, not something she had always been sure of, and then her real life could begin.

The last two years, Mother had not been able to beat Grace with the same energy and zest. Mother had a heart condition now.

"Because it's so black," Grace said to Janice, still her only confidant.

Mother's heart developed what the family doctor called arrhythmia. At times it beat wildly, as though it was trying to leave her chest. Grace could see the pulse pounding in her neck. Their small town had only one doctor, and Dr.

Flanagan treated everything. He prescribed pills, but Mother didn't like to take medicine. She had no faith in it; said it made her feel peculiar. She preferred her own herbal remedies, sending Grace out into the yard to pick various leaves and berries to brew into bitter tea. Mother pinched her nose shut and swallowed it, but it didn't seem to be helping. She was skeletal in her thinness now. Her feet and legs sometimes swelled alarmingly and her rattling cough woke Grace at night.

But she was still mean. She no longer had the strength to rain blows upon Grace, or yank her hair or surprise her with a sucker punch in the stomach, but she could talk. Grace sometimes thought the words hurt more than the blows.

"Little whore," she'd hiss in Grace's ear in the middle of the night. When Grace's eyes flew open in alarm, Mother's contorted face would be inches from her own. "Think I don't know what you're doing with the boys? Oh, I know, I know you are rotten to the bone. When you have a kid, that spawn will be rotten just like you. You were born bad and you'll die bad, and everything you touch will be ruined."

The hate-filled words went on, sometimes for hours. When morning finally came, and Mother fell into bed, exhausted, Grace got dressed and took herself to school, red-eyed and silent. But now escape was within reach. Her father had left her a life-insurance policy, left it in trust to her alone in a moment of prescience, to be available on her eighteenth birthday. That was just days away. With that money, she'd buy her freedom.

Grace sent for college application forms, but Mother burned them as soon as they arrived. Mrs. Winechester offered Grace the use of her address at school, perhaps in guilty atonement for the aid she'd failed to give years earlier. So Grace was able to apply to the big state university two hundred miles from home - too far for Mother to get to, even had she still been driving. When the acceptance letter arrived,

Grace knew all she had to do was endure one more summer.

She'd dreamed of the day she could leave home since she was a little girl, but now that the time had almost come, she found herself in a maelstrom of conflicting emotions. Freedom, peace, education, a better life, those were her goals, she told herself. But home, Mother—that was what she knew, and while it was bad, it was familiar. College was unknown. She was both excited and scared at the prospect of going there.

She didn't dare acknowledge to herself a niggling little feeling, so stupid, she told herself, that she tried not to allow it to surface. But sometimes, late at night, it surfaced anyway: maybe, someday, she'd find the right formula, say the right words, look the right way - and then Mother would change. She'd become the warm, loving mom for whom Grace longed. If she left home, it would never happen.

There were no relatives to applaud when Grace crossed the stage and received her high-school diploma. Mother laughed harshly at the very idea of attending the ceremony. Janice's family clapped and cheered loyally, their voices lonely in the auditorium. It didn't matter. The next day Grace would celebrate her eighteenth birthday by visiting Mr. Moeller, the family's insurance agent, and finding out how to cash in her policy.

She could hardly wait until nine o'clock, when the office opened. She was on the stoop when Mr. Moeller arrived, and she stepped aside politely so he could unlock the door. He looked puzzled to see her.

"Now then, Grace, what brings you out so early in the morning? By the way, congratulations on graduating in the top ten percent of your class. I read the article in the paper. Are you looking for a job? We might have something for a smart young lady like you, part-time clerical right now, but it could lead to full-time."

"No, Mr. Moeller, I'm not looking for a job, but thank you. I've come to see about the insurance policy my Dad left me. It was to come to me on my eighteenth birthday, and that's today."

Mr. Moeller stopped in mid-stride. "Your insurance policy? Grace, your mother cashed that in years ago."

"What? How was she allowed to do that? It was left to me only. My Dad told me so before he died."

"That's true, but your mother petitioned the court to release the funds to her. She pleaded poverty and said she didn't have enough money to send you to high school or pay your doctor bills. Did she not tell you at the time?"

~*~

"Mother, how could you? You knew Dad meant for me to use that insurance money to go to college. How could you take it and never even tell me?"

Her mother threw back her head, her white throat showing every cartilage, and laughed for a long time. "Just finding that out, are you? Surprise, surprise. Your father could have had no idea that you'd turn out to be a wretched brat. If he'd known, he'd never have left you a dime. I can just see you up at that fancy college. You'd be laughed at for being ugly and stupid, and you'd take up with some trashy boy and get yourself pregnant, and then who'd have to take care of you and your brat?"

"But...you hate me...don't you want to get me off your hands?"

"I certainly do hate you - everyone does, but I won't inflict you on the world. You stay right here where I can give you what you deserve. Oh, and by the way, I still have the money, but you won't get your greedy paws on it. Just know it's there. Maybe someday, if you try real hard, you can earn it back." Mother laughed again at the thought.

Grace withdrew from college, having never gone a day, and then she withdrew from life. Left to herself, she wouldn't have bothered to get out of bed, but Mother made sure she was up. Sometimes there was an icy cascade of water over her head at three in the morning; sometimes she gasped her way out from under a pillow pressed on her face; sometimes her old bicycle horn blasted in her ear. Mother enjoyed finding new ways to remind Grace that she lived in hell and always would.

I'm bigger than she is, and stronger, and she's sick now. Why do I let her do these things to me? But the little girl who still lived inside Grace's head recoiled in terror at the idea of fighting back. Mother would kill her, for sure. Safer to be very, very still.

That afternoon Mother dozed in her recliner. Grace waited until she heard snores, then slipped out the door. She headed straight for the library, where she was well known and liked for her quiet, studious ways.

"I'd like to do some studying at home," she said to the librarian, "since I can't go to school after all."

"I just hate that for you, dear. Of course you should try to keep learning. What can I do to help you?"

Grace asked for books on history, mathematics and science at the level of a college freshman, and managed to get home and hide her armload of tomes before her mother awakened. She hoped Mother wouldn't go on one of her rampages, find the books and destroy them. The last time that happened, she'd had to turn over her earnings from after-school jobs for months to pay back the library. Taking the science book with her, she climbed up to her old hiding place in the cherry tree, and began to read. The first section was titled "Natural Science: Plants and Flowers."

There were still a lot of flowers in the neglected yard. Long ago, when Mother had been more nearly normal, she and Grace's father had taken an interest in their garden. Now the scraggly remnants of the hardiest of those old plants hung on. The enormous hydrangeas bloomed valiantly every summer. Tangled rose vines produced a few flowers each year before reverting to naked, thorny canes. Black-eyed Susan came back stubbornly, persisting in the weed-choked beds. The wild flower and herb garden had been a special project of Grace's father. There were chicory and foxglove, sweet William and yarrow, monkshood and Johnny-jump-up. Sage, rosemary, basil, fennel and other herbs she couldn't identify grew despite weeds and neglect. Grace read about the ones she knew by name.

Gazing down at her father's garden, she paused for a long time after she read about monkshood. The entire plant was poisonous, the book said, especially the leaves and roots. Ingested or absorbed through the skin, the poison acted rapidly and caused nausea, vomiting, paralysis of the respiratory system, and ultimately, cardiac failure. Grace descended from the tree and cast the text into the deepest recesses of her closet.

~*~

Grace went back to the insurance office and asked Mr. Moeller if he really could let her have a part-time job. He looked with concern at her white face and told her that he certainly could, and she could start tomorrow if she wanted.

"Thank you, Mr. Moeller, I'll do the best I can for you. I need to save for college now that Dad's insurance money is gone."

"I feel real bad about that, Grace," Mr. Moeller said. "I had no idea your mother had not discussed it with you."

"Of course not, how could you know? I'm going to study at home, so when I do get the tuition together, I won't be out of the habit."

Mr. Moeller had heard rumors about what went on in Grace's home. That the child had kept her sanity and was willing to work for her own salvation seemed miraculous to him. Under her studious exterior, he sensed the presence of an implacable will. She was only a girl, but somehow she was a force to be reckoned with. He'd known her father. He'd do whatever he could for the daughter now.

CHAPTER SIX

2014

Lavender sometimes felt that she'd left her body and been transformed into her mother. Despite her beauty, she wasn't vain about her appearance, and contentedly slouched around her childhood home in her mother's old clothes. They swam on her, disguising her reed-slimness. With her hair scraped back in a ponytail, and a face bare of make-up, Lavender looked like a teen-ager got up as a little old lady. That suited her fine. She'd had enough of being a glamour girl. The less she looked like her old self, the better.

Lavender was hiding out. Her split with Kevin, the latest in a long string of beaus, was not amicable. Their relationship had started promisingly. Kevin had been proud of her, parading her around town, reveling in the attention she always drew when she wanted to. He urged her to move in with him until finally, when she had the opportunity to sublet her apartment for a year and bring in a little cash, she did.

But once she was living in his house, things changed. He no longer wanted to go out. Then he resisted having friends in. Her every phone call and errand was followed up with a quiz. He checked the mileage on the car before and after her trips. Her friends were not welcome. Her sister was not welcome. He said it was because he wanted her all to himself, that he wanted their love affair to be everything and the only thing in their lives. Lavender, characteristically, took the path of least resistance. It was easier to go along.

It happened so gradually she hardly noticed the lessening of contacts, the constriction of horizons. There were unexpected treats to distract her: bouquets of flowers, bottles of wine, surprise trips to the seashore. But one day Lavender woke up and realized that she hadn't talked to anyone but Kevin in weeks. She rose, showered, dressed, and headed for the door.

"Where are you going?" he demanded in the truculent tone that had become the new normal.

"I thought I'd go see Martha today. Haven't seen her in ages."

"I don't like you seeing Martha, you know that. She's not a good influence on you."

"K-Kevin, she's my s-sister. I can see her whenever I w-want."

"You're my girlfriend, and I pay your way. You do as I say."

Lavender reached for the doorknob. The blow was so unexpected that it spun her around. She fell heavily, hitting her head on the floor with a sickening thunk. Dazed, she lay still, trying to collect her senses. A kick in the ribs doubled her over into a ball. Instinctively, she put her arms around her head to protect it. But there were no more blows or kicks. Instead, she heard the door slam, felt the floor vibrate with that slam. Kevin's car started up with a roar, and tires screeched as he raced away.

Groaning, she raised herself to a sitting position, holding her head, swiping at the blood running from her nose. *Got to get up, got to get out of here before he comes back.* He'd taken the car, so she'd have to walk to the bus stop and catch the bus to—where? She thought of calling her sister to come and get her, but somehow, she didn't want Martha to know about this. It was too humiliating.

Struggling to her feet, she made her way to the bedroom. Kevin kept a secret supply of cash in the pocket of an old overcoat in the closet. He didn't know she knew about it. She plunged her bloody hand into the pocket and withdrew a wad of bills. Yes, this would be enough. She'd call a taxi and go to the airport. He wouldn't be expecting her to have the means to run. She'd buy a ticket at random, a ticket to any place not here. And she'd hide.

~*~

Lavender blessed modern technology that enabled her to reconnect with Martha while giving her sister no idea that she was out of town. Text messages and cell phone calls could be sent from anywhere, and they left no trail. It seemed important that Martha not know what Kevin had done. Lavender was ashamed that she had chosen so poorly, embarrassed by the need to be bailed out yet again. Holed up in an Econo-Lodge in Butte, Montana, healing from her bruises, she tried to think what to do next.

The news of their mother's death came in Martha's choked voice on her cell phone. "Where are you?" she wailed. "Nobody answered the door when I went to Kevin's house. It looks like nobody even lives there anymore."

"I've been out of t-town for a few days but I'll come back today. I'll l-let you know what time my plane gets in. Can you p-pick me up at the airport?"

"Of course, I will. But what about Kevin?"

"He's away on a b-business trip. He'll be gone for another m-month."

~*~

After the funeral, it was easiest for Lavender to remain in her childhood home. She knew her days there were numbered because Martha was getting more and more impatient to put the house on the market. The sisters had agreed from the start that they wouldn't be one of those families that fought over an inheritance. Their mother's medical bills had pretty well taken all her money, anyway, and the house was the only major asset left. Lavender understood it wasn't fair to deprive Martha of her share of its value, but she felt a lassitude that pinned her in place. There'd always been a man waiting to whirl her away from the troublesome aspects of life, like making a living. But now there was only Kevin, and the thought of him made her shiver.

She hadn't seen him since he'd beat her, but she'd dreamed about him the night before. He was scratching at her bedroom window, trying to get in, trying to get to her. She'd awakened with a swallowed scream to see the branches of the maple tree tapping gently at the panes. Unable to go back to sleep, she'd wandered through the dark house, peering carefully around the curtains at the dark yard. She thought she saw a shadowy figure duck behind the hedge, but no; she was just jumpy from the dream. She comforted herself with the thought that Kevin didn't know where she was. He'd never wanted to meet her mother, so he'd not been here, to the house.

Nevertheless, Lavender looked around for a hidey-hole, just in case. It was an old habit from her childhood, rooted in the days when she hid in the nooks and crannies her father had built. Her mother became accustomed to looking for her in the linen closet or behind the lattice that skirted the porch. Once she'd crawled into a tiny recess behind a closet and fallen asleep. When she emerged, rubbing her eyes and yawning, the house was full of policemen, and her mother was hysterical.

Somehow, that old habit had translated into an adult need to keep an escape hatch always in mind. She searched the familiar house. In closets, under beds, behind long draperies - those hiding places were no good for a grown woman. She thought about the basement but there was no way out except the one flight of stairs. She'd be trapped down there, and being underground made her skin crawl. That left the attic, with her Dad's goofy bookcase stairway leading up to it. When the girls were little, they were strictly forbidden to play on those steps. Lavender remembered one of the few spankings she'd ever gotten was because she'd disobeyed. She and her mother had both cried afterward.

"Why did you have to build such a dangerous thing right in our home?" Lavender's mother sobbed to her father.

"Now, Grace, how often do we ever go into the attic? This way, you can use the bookcases every day and on the rare occasions that we need to go up there, we'll just be very careful. The girls can learn to stay off them. It's good for them to have limits."

It was a precarious climb, especially if you were hauling storage boxes. You had to hug the wall, and be careful where you put your feet. She wondered how her father had ever managed with the big, black trunk.

Once I get up there, though, I could close the trap door, and sit on it. And then no one could get into the attic. I'd be safe.

Lavender mulled over the idea as she lay in bed that night. Too drowsy to think of the hitches in this brilliant plan, she was able to sleep. The next morning, in the bright light of day, the whole idea seemed ludicrous. But she didn't quite forget it.

Inspired by the sunshine flooding into the kitchen window, Lavender resolved that today was the day, the day she'd take hold of things. She'd begin by clearing out her mother's closet. Determinedly, she opened the door, and reached for the light switch. But the smell of *Chanel Number Five*, her mother's one extravagance, stopped her short. A predictable birthday gift from her father, the fragrance was her mother's signature scent. It was imprinted on her children from pre-memory, from pre-birth, maybe. Lavender's eyes filled with tears, and she sank down on the bed.

~*~

Martha found her asleep when she stopped by later that afternoon. All the doors were unlocked when she arrived, and the house was eerily quiet. She tiptoed through the rooms until she found Lavender on her mother's bed.

"Wake up, Lavender," she said, shaking her sister's shoulder.

"Oh...was I asleep? I didn't mean to fall asleep." With a huge yawn, Lavender stretched. Her eyes fluttered shut again.

"Come *on*," Martha said impatiently, shaking her sister harder. "It's three in the afternoon. You don't need to be sleeping now; you'll never sleep tonight. Get up, and I'll fix us some tea."

Settled at the kitchen table, the sisters regarded each other over their teacups. Lavender's blue-black hair escaped from a sloppy up-do, and curled around her face. It should have looked awful, Martha thought, but it just looked endearing, all those little tendrils and curls around her ears. Lavender wore a shapeless shift that had belonged to their mother, and no shoes. Martha was dressed in spotless white Bermudas and a pink-checked shirt, with a white sweater thrown casually around her shoulders. Every hair of her sensible, short hair-do was in place. She wore make-up and perfume, and knew in her heart that she didn't look one-tenth as enticing as Lavender. *Lav, Lav, pee-pot Lav*, she thought, then was horrified at herself for violating the old taboo, if only in her mind. This was her little sister, after all, left in her care. Martha didn't take her responsibilities lightly, and that's why she was here: to issue a warning.

"Lavender, I think I might have seen Kevin today," she said.

"What? Kevin? Where?"

"When I came out of the market, there was a man looking in the windows of my car. He was wearing a hoodie, so I couldn't see his face. I yelled, 'Hey!' and he ran. When he did, just something in the way he moved made me think, why, that's Kevin. I'm still not one hundred percent positive it was him—but I think it was."

"Oh, no. He's looking for me," Lavender said.

"Why? What the heck is going on? I know you said you broke up with him, but why is he looking for you? Do you owe him money?"

"Yeah, I guess I do." Lavender gave a short laugh. "But he's not after money. He's after me. I ran away from him. When I said we broke up, I didn't t-tell you everything."

"You'd better tell me now."

"He changed after I moved in with him," Lavender said. "He didn't want me to have any friends, or see you, or go out of the house without him. I only had a little money from the renters in my apartment, but he'd watch for the mail, and grab that check when it came. He said I owed it to him for room and board." She hung her head, and whispered the next words: "He b-beat me up. That's when I left."

"Oh, Lavender! Damn him! I never liked him. You should have come straight to me, and then we could have called the police."

"I was so scared; all I could think of was getting away. I took a taxi to the airport, and flew to Butte, Montana."

"Montana? We don't know a soul there."

"That's exactly why I chose it. I figured the more random, the better. Less chance that Kevin would figure it out. And he didn't. I'd probably still be there if Mom hadn't died. But he doesn't know anything about that."

"He might. Her obituary was in the newspaper. He'd have recognized the name, and he'd know you'd be here for the funeral."

Lavender instinctively looked at the window, as if expecting to see Kevin's face there. "But this is my safe p-place," she said softly.

"So that's why you didn't want to leave. You've been hiding here," Martha said. "That's why you don't care how you look, and don't want to sell the house. Why didn't you just tell me?"

"I get tired of being the hard-luck sister," Lavender said. "You're so perfect, with your sweet husband and perfect kids and beautiful home. And I'm just - just nothing. I never could compete with you."

"Are you kidding? You're the beauty, I'm the drudge. You were always Mom's favorite. I've been jealous of *you* since the day you were born."

They looked at each other. The corners of Martha's mouth twitched. Lavender's eyes crinkled at the corners. The next moment, they were laughing.

"You're such a damn goody two-shoes!" Lavender gasped.

"You're Lav, Lav, Pee-Pot Lav!" Martha got out, tears of hilarity streaming down her face.

"I love you, Martha," Lavender said, mopping her eyes.

"I love you, too, Pee-Pot. And now we have to figure out what to do about Kevin."

CHAPTER SEVEN

1970

Grace had a beau. In spite of everything, there was a boy who was willing to brave her crazy home life. Thomas Allen McGuire didn't come from an Ozzie and Harriett home himself. His father was the town tippler and his mother cleaned the big homes of the wealthy to put food on the table for Tommy and his sister. She learned to race from her job directly to the grocery store, pay in hand. Otherwise, it went to the Shamrock Pub. So Tommy had some idea of hardships at home.

He was waiting for her one day when she got off work, standing on the corner near the insurance office. Grace's middle-school crush on Tommy had been drowned in abuse from her mother when she'd found out about it. No boy is worth a beating, Grace'd thought at the time. But she remembered how she'd written his name over and over in her notebook. Now they had both graduated from high school and were working and saving. He'd be headed off to university in the fall.

"Hi, Grace," he said, falling into step beside her.

"Tommy, what are you doing here?"

"Just thought I'd walk you home, see how you're doing this summer."

"Oh, okay. I'm doing fine, I guess. How about you?"

"I'm working at the filling station, saving everything I can for school. Say, I can't offer much in the way of a date, but would you like to take a walk after supper? Maybe stop for a Coke, or something?"

"Uh, sure, I'd like that. But my mother – it's hard to get away sometimes."

"Yeah, I understand. Tell you what: I'll wait for you at the drugstore at seven. If you can't make it, I won't be mad, or anything."

"Could you make it seven-thirty? Mother always watches *Gunsmoke* at seven-thirty on Thursdays, and a lot of times she falls asleep. I don't know how I'd get through the evenings if she didn't watch television."

Grace had been surprised when Mother bought a television set. The big wooden console brought the outside world into their claustrophobic home. Mother watched it incessantly, and Grace was grateful for the lull in hostilities.

Only when her rage at Grace was boiling did Mother turn off the set. There were evenings when she made Grace sit opposite her as she screamed abuse until her hoarse voice failed. Sometimes Grace would see Tommy walk by as she sat there. With all the windows open in the summer, her mother's voice was clearly audible outside the house. Tommy's shoulders would hunch as he kept walking. They'd discussed it, he and Grace, and she'd told him any attempt on his part to rescue her would only make her life worse.

"Why do you take it?" he'd asked. "Just get up and walk

out. Come to me. Or let me come in and get you. I'm not afraid of her."

"But I am," Grace confessed. "I'm still so scared of her. Even though she's old and sick now, you can't imagine how powerful she is. I swear, she can read my mind. She'd stop at nothing to hurt me if I ever dared defy her. I don't know why she hates me, why she wants to keep me at home, but I'm not sure I'll ever have the courage to leave while she's alive."

~*~

The smell of smoke penetrated Grace's sleep. It was hard to stir, to struggle to sit up on the edge of the bed. When she did, her head exploded with pain. Eyes stinging, she groped her way to the door. When she opened it, smoke billowed into the room. Coughing and retching, she felt her way along the wall to the window. It was a dormer set in the peak of the slanting roof, and it was wide open to the summer night. She pushed away the screen and stuck her head outside, gulping in the humid night air. As the smoke thickened, she climbed out onto the roof.

Mother, she thought, *Mother's trapped inside*. She slid down the shingles, catching herself on the drain spout. Her old friend, the cherry tree, reached a generous branch over the roof and on it she climbed down to the ground. Racing around to the locked front door, she pounded on it, shouting for her mother. Lights went on in the neighbors' houses. A few people stumbled out sleepily to see what was going on.

"Call the Fire Department!" Grace shouted. "There's a fire. Mother's inside."

"No, she's not," one neighbor said, pointing. "She's standing right here."

Grace turned and met Mother's eyes. There was triumph in them, just discernible for an instant before Mother clutched her throat and coughed convincingly.

"I managed to get out," she croaked, "but then I collapsed."

Mother was surrounded by neighbors, seated on a porch step and given a glass of water as approaching sirens grew louder. The firefighters wasted no time in applying their axes to the front door. They swept through the house, emerging a few minutes later carrying a metal bucket that glowed red.

"Here's the fire," one of them said. "It's contained in this bucket, although it wouldn't have been for much longer. It would have burned through the bottom and caught the carpet on fire. This was deliberately set."

Mother rose to her feet and pointed to Grace. "She must have done it. She's trying to kill me."

~*~

"Now, Grace, calm down. Nobody believes for a minute that you set that fire." Dr. Flanagan spoke soothingly. "We know – I know – what your mother is like. She's my patient, for whatever it's worth. She's not been taking her medicine, has she?"

"I don't think so. She brews tea from herbs that she makes me bring in from the back yard. She doesn't trust medicine, she says."

"I've known your mother all my life. In fact, we went through all twelve years of elementary and high school in the same class. I'm going to be very frank, Grace. She was always a troubled soul; she was just plain mean as a kid. I remember she was questioned about the deaths of some small animals when we were in the fifth grade. A couple of kittens...well, you don't need to know that.

"What I'm saying," Dr. Flanagan continued, "is that she's a sick woman, mentally and physically. Now she has heart failure on top of dementia. It's especially hard to cope with because some of her behavior is willful and some is the product of her deteriorating mental condition. She's not going to get any better, but she could live quite a while yet. Have you considered admitting her to a care facility?"

"She'd never go and I couldn't make her," Grace said. "She wants to be at home where she can get at me. I mean, be with me."

"I know about the abuse, too, Grace. There's no need to pretend with me."

"If you know...if you've known all these years...why have you never done anything to help me? Why has no one ever tried to help me?"

"Oh, Grace. I did try. I talked to you mother about it on several occasions. She denied everything and never allowed me to see what was happening for myself. Short of knocking down your door and demanding to see your bruises, what could I do? As for the neighbors and such, well, folks around here think that a child is her family's business. They don't like nosing into the way someone is raising their own." At her incredulous look, he added, "I guess none of those reasons make sense to you."

"No," Grace said, "but it reminds me that I am on my own, always have been and always will be. If my problems are ever solved, it will be me solving them."

~*~

When Tommy headed off to college in the fall, Grace felt her aloneness more than ever. Since the fire, she was afraid to close her eyes at night lest she never open them again. Locking and barricading her door kept Mother out, but there was always the possibility of another fire. Grace hid all the matches, but Mother had money and she was still able to walk to the corner store.

Mother had taken to minor acts of sabotage, like hiding Grace's purse, cutting off her shoestrings, removing the light bulbs form all the lamps in her room. These relatively minor annoyances were done with persistence and ingenuity, and they wore Grace down.

Inside, she still felt like the little girl who was allowed to use as many Band-Aids as necessary to cover the welts. It remained vitally important to hide what Mother did. If Grace wasn't there, Mother wouldn't be able to cope. Outsiders would come in, and they'd find out what Mother really was. Something terrible would happen.

Her thoughts raced in futile circles. It was impossible to turn them off, especially on nights when she sensed that Mother was planning some new hell. Then she tried to stay awake all night, to be on guard. Dragging herself to work the next morning, seeing the look of pity on Mr. Moeller's face, she felt helpless and hopeless.

CHAPTER EIGHT

2014

Lavender's head whipped around as her eye caught a familiar figure. Could that be....? Yes. Kevin stood on the other side of the street. He'd turned his back to study a store window, but she knew him. Breathlessly, she turned and ran, dodging other pedestrians. When she reached her mother's car, the one she drove nowadays, she turned and her eyes raked the area in all directions. She didn't see him.

Maybe I was mistaken, she told herself, entering the car and quickly locking the doors. She turned the key, checked the side mirror and saw Kevin reflected in it. With a muffled shriek, she jerked the car into drive, rode up over the curb and bounced down again, taking off with a squeal of rubber.

It wasn't the first time she'd spotted him lately. He'd been in the neighbor's backyard one morning. When she opened the curtains he was just standing there, looking toward the house with a little smile on his face. Before she could react, he was gone, melting into the shrubbery.

She'd heard the doorbell at three A.M. one night. It

triggered the porch light, but when she peered fearfully through the window, no one was there. There were phone calls. When she answered, she'd hear his voice. He'd say, "Hi, just checking on you. I'll be over soon. Leave the door unlocked." Or he'd unleash a torrent of profanity and threats that left her shaking. Or he'd just breathe.

He followed her to the supermarket, standing across the parking lot when she left the store. She found a single rose on the back step one morning, a dead mouse the next. A note appeared under the windshield wiper while the car was shut up in the garage. It said, "I'm watching. We'll get together soon."

Once, and this was the scariest of all, she'd reached into her underwear drawer, and felt a piece of paper. It said, "I see you still wear the same kind of panties." In horror, she grabbed the entire contents of the drawer and threw it in the washer. He'd touched her most intimate possessions. He'd been in the house. Was no place safe from him?

Lavender's nerves were shot. Her slim frame became gaunt and her beautiful eyes were red-rimmed from lack of sleep. The stutter, a life-long barometer of stress, was back, more pronounced than ever. Of course, Martha noticed.

"What are we going to do with you, Lavender?" she said.

"I d-don't know what to d-do with myself."

Lavender didn't tell Martha about the times she practiced climbing the slippery bookshelf stairs to the attic as fast as she could, slamming the trapdoor shut behind her, and sitting on it. She didn't tell her that she'd stockpiled some bottles of water and a few energy bars up there. That she'd carried up a pillow and blanket, just in case. It seemed too survivalist and crazy. Besides, maybe Kevin would get tired of stalking her soon. Maybe he'd just go away.

Kevin had flexible hours because he worked from home, going into the office only once or twice a week. That was the blessing and the curse of being a computer wizard. He was extremely productive pecking away at the keyboard in his den with no interruptions, but his social skills, not great to begin with, languished in the isolation.

Kevin bragged that he was so valuable to his employer that he could get away with anything. Offers from other companies came to him on a regular basis, but he said he couldn't be bothered with the hassle of changing jobs. He made plenty of money where he was; he felt no impetus to change.

She'd observed first-hand that Kevin was extremely strict about certain things. For instance, the house had to be spotlessly clean at all times. When her feet hit the floor in the morning, she'd best turn right around and make the bed. No dirty dishes in the sink, ever. Laundry was done daily, and chlorine bleach was the predominant scent in the house.

Kevin was equally strict about her appearance. A weekly manicure and pedicure were required. She got her hair done frequently, shaved her legs every night, and knew better than to step out the door looking anything but perfect. Her closet was stuffed with designer clothing, some still wearing price tags. He expected her to dress up just to hang around the house after he'd stopped letting her go out.

Kevin set himself work goals every day, and if night came before he accomplished them, he worked obsessively until sunrise. Control - of his environment, of his work, and of her - was paramount with him. Lavender was ill-equipped to deal with it. Passive by nature, accustomed to her beauty smoothing every path, she simply gave in. Perhaps, like all bullies, he would have backed down had she been able to defy him. She could not. Running away from him, leaving his house, hiding out—that took every bit of Lavender's resources. In the face of his persistent stalking, she felt terrified and helpless. She tried to explain all this to Martha.

"You d-don't know him," Lavender said. "He's relentless. And he doesn't m-mind hurting me."

"You're right, I don't know him very well at all," Martha said. "But I know about bullies. They fold if you have the guts to stand up to them. And I know you. You are not the person to do it, because he's got you spooked. I'm not afraid of him. Let me handle Kevin."

"I can't let you d-do that," Lavender began, but Martha cut her off.

"Okay, let's think about your alternatives. Do you want to call the police? I think that's a good idea, actually. Then there'd be a public record of what Kevin is doing."

"Not the p-police!" Lavender said. "I d-don't want to involve them."

"Why not?"

"You never know wh-what they'll do. M-maybe they'd arrest *me*."

"Why would they?"

Lavender was silent. She looked out the window, and twisted the rings on her fingers. Finally, she said, "There m-might be a warrant."

"A warrant! Why?"

"K-Kevin said I stole from him, and he filed a complaint with the p-police. That's what he t-told me on the phone."

"But that's a false accusation! He can't do that."

"I d-did take his money. That's what I used to run away. He's s-smart, isn't he? Now I'm scared to report him."

~*~

Martha stomped up the front steps of Kevin's house, heels hitting hard, and leaned on the doorbell. She heard it chime deep inside the house. When the door didn't open instantly, she leaned on the bell again. Finally, footsteps approached, the doorknob turned, and he appeared. He looked her up and down.

"Well, well, Martha. What can I do for you today?"

"You can leave my sister alone."

"Ah. Do you see her here? And I'm not wherever she is. So I'd say I *am* leaving her alone." His smirk made her clench her fists.

"Look, let's not play games. You've been stalking her. We both know Lavender is too gentle a soul to do what needs to be done to you."

"And what would that be, Martha?"

"A swift kick in the balls springs to mind."

"Oh, I see. You're threatening me? Bodily harm and all that? Terroristic threats? The police might want to add that to their report. Crime seems to run in the family. I've already warned them that Lavender is a thief, and that she carries a gun. I suggested they might want to have their tasers ready."

"Kevin, you son of a bitch. Can't you man up and accept the fact that Lavender is through with you? Surely you can find some other woman to beat up."

"Maybe so, maybe so. Are you applying for the job?"

"Listen to me. Leave. Lavender. Alone."

"*You* listen to *me*. Mind. Your. Own. Business."

Neither of them would break eye contact. Finally, she turned and walked to her car, Kevin's laughter following her.

When she glanced back at him as she drove away, she saw that he was still laughing, waving goodbye with his middle finger extended. Martha felt fury that burned like dry ice.

"Oh yes, my friend," she said aloud. "Wait for it, because it's coming. You might be able to bully Lavender, but you haven't tangled with me yet."

Her hands shaking with angry energy, her brain ticking over smoothly as adrenaline enhanced the synapses, Martha was making plans. She could hardly wait to implement them.

She drove directly to Pat's house. Throwing the car in park, she was up the steps, and knocking on the door in one fluid motion. She cut through Pat's flustered response to her unexpected visit, saying, "Aunt Pat, listen. I need your help. Lavender needs your help."

Pat became still. "I knew it," she said. "I knew there was something wrong when I saw Lavender looking the way she did the last time she was here to work on the quilt. Her hands were so shaky she couldn't thread a needle. And she made terrible stitches that I had to rip out after she left. Her stutter was back, too. What's wrong? Is she sick?"

"Sick at heart, maybe, but no, she's healthy otherwise. Lavender is being stalked by an ex-boyfriend. Do you remember Kevin? Lavender lived with him until he slugged her one day. She left him, and now he's literally driving her crazy, showing up wherever she goes, watching her from the yard—he's even been inside the house."

"Oh, the poor child. She must be terrified. Have you called the police?"

"He prevented that by filing a police report first, saying that Lavender stole from him. Now she's scared to involve the authorities for fear they will arrest her. Kevin's smart, no doubt about that. Lavender can't handle this alone, Aunt Pat. We have to help her."

"Of course. I'll do whatever I can."

"Good. Because I have a plan. Lavender needs to get out of the house, to a safe place Kevin doesn't know about. Will you let her come here?"

"Certainly, I will. You don't need to ask."

"He may track her down. I don't want to minimize the danger. His behavior has escalated over the last few weeks, and I can't predict what he might do."

Pat smiled. She motioned Martha to follow her, and led the way through an aisle in the clutter to a small, black safe almost hidden among the flotsam and jetsam of her "collections." Twirling the dial, she opened the door, and extracted a compact Smith and Wesson nine millimeter automatic.

"And I have a permit to carry it, too," she said proudly. "I learned to shoot in the military. I didn't want to be alone and defenseless in a house filled with treasures."

Martha glanced around at the piles and mounds of miscellaneous stuff. *One man's trash*, she thought. Pat picked up her weapon and thrust it deep into the pocket of her roomy pants.

"Bring him on," she said. "I'm ready."

CHAPTER NINE

1972

Grace's head nestled on Tommy's shoulder as they lay on an army blanket hidden in the tall grass. They were naked and blissful in the aftermath of making love.

"It won't be long now, Grace," Tommy said. "We're both twenty, not teenagers any longer. I've only got one more year to go in school. Once I've got my degree, we'll get married and start our real lives."

"I just hope I can last that long," Grace said. "Mother is wearing me down. I may die before she does."

"Don't say that," Tommy said, his finger to her lips. "We'll make it. Be strong for me, darling."

Grace couldn't find the words to tell him that her period was a month overdue. A whole month--that had never happened before. The summer had been full of long, languorous nights under the stars on this very blanket. Because they were both saving fiercely for their future, they didn't spend money on movies or dinners. Being alone together was enough, but it inevitably led to sex. Could she be pregnant? It was too soon to know; she wouldn't mention it to Tommy yet. Maybe it was a false alarm. Grace shivered in fear.

"Cold, honey?" Tommy asked. "Here, let me warm you up."

~*~

"Ah, there you are, you slut," Mother said, when Grace arrived home.

She was almost always asleep when Grace got in late at night, but tonight she was not only awake, but wide awake. She looked gleeful. That was the word that came to Grace's mind as she warily scanned her mother's face.

"Guess what I didn't find in your bathroom?" Mother said.

Oh, no, she's been going through my things again, Grace thought. She knew better than to react, but if Mother had been snooping in Grace's room, that was serious. What if she found the bank book with each month's savings carefully recorded? Grace would put nothing past her mother, including her ability to somehow steal from the bank. After all, she'd managed to steal Grace's inheritance from her father.

"I didn't find any signs that you've had your monthly lately," Mother went on. "Which you should have had. I keep track, you know. You can't fool me, missy. So I guess it's finally happened. You've finally managed to spawn. I've known for years you'd end up pregnant. You're nothing but a whore, a slut, a...."

Grace stopped listening, panic beating in her ears like birds' wings. What if she really was carrying Tommy's child? No baby could be safe in this house. *She* wasn't safe, and would be even less so if Mother was proven right about her pregnancy.

~*~

She didn't make an appointment, just showed up in Dr. Flanagan's office at nine the next morning, and said she'd wait until he had time for her. An old-fashioned physician, he still kept Saturday morning office hours. She had to wait until eleven, but finally the last patient had been seen, and she was alone among the year-old copies of National Geographic.

"Dr. Flanagan will see you now," said the nurse, whom Grace had known since they were both in elementary school. She detected the look of sympathy behind the professional demeanor, and guessed she wasn't the first single girl to make an unscheduled visit to the doctor.

The exam was excruciatingly embarrassing. If she'd had the means, she'd have traveled to another place, seen any other doctor. Grace had known Dr. Flanagan all her life. He'd treated her childhood illnesses, but not her injuries. Mother wouldn't allow that. She willed her mind away from the narrow, high table with its cold metal stirrups, just as she'd learned to will it away from other unpleasant experiences. The exam completed, she dressed and joined Dr. Flanagan as instructed in his cluttered little office.

"Well, Grace," he said, "I don't know whether you'll be glad or sad about this, but you're pregnant. About two and a half months, I'd say. You and Tommy?"

"Yes. Me and Tommy. We're planning to get married as soon as he finishes school."

"Lots of people speed up the wedding date when a little one is on the way. No shame in that. There's married housing at college. My wife and I lived in it."

"I'm sure we could manage. It's Mother, you see. Who will take care of her if I move out?"

"You can't defer your life indefinitely for your mother, especially one as undeserving..." Dr. Flanagan caught himself. "I know you can make a good decision about this, Grace. I've seen you grow up. You're a courageous, intelligent girl—woman, now. If I can be of any help to you, let me know. But be careful. Your mother has shown herself to be dangerous. You have another life to protect now."

~*~

Grace's mind simply refused to address what to do next. She desperately needed to talk to Tommy, but he was at school, and wouldn't be home again until the Thanksgiving break. She thought of writing him a letter, but it seemed ridiculously impersonal. Telling him that he was going to be a father as he stood at the hall phone in the dorm surrounded by passing classmates seemed the worst way to break this news.

The baby was already precious to Grace. Among all the things she wasn't sure about, one fact stood up straight and tall: she wanted this baby. She longed to be a good mother, the mother she never had. Maybe, as she nurtured her own child, she could also nurture the terrified little girl who still lived inside her. Maybe she could teach *her* not to be so afraid.

Meanwhile, Mother wore a crazy grin and muttered to herself like some storybook crone. When Grace entered the room, she sang *Rockabye Baby* in a cracked voice that sent chills up Grace's spine. Once again, she turned to Janice.

"What am I going to do?" she asked her.

"Why, you're going to marry Tommy just like you planned, only a little early. And you two will go back to college and live in married housing, and he'll get his degree, and you'll have the baby and you'll live happily ever after."

"I wish it was that simple! What am I going to do about Mother?"

"Why do you have to do anything about her?"

"She's not fit to stay alone," Grace said. "She's apt to burn the house down, or starve if nobody fixes her meals."

"And that would be a good thing," Janice said crisply. She'd had years of seeing Grace's bruised body and mind. There was no sympathy left in her for Grace's abuser.

"But she's not in her right mind," Grace said. "I know she's a horror—no one knows that better than I—but she's old and sick now. How can I just leave her?"
"Grace, are you safe in her house?"

"Well...not entirely."

"Then your baby isn't safe, either. Are you willing to let your child be exposed to a life of abuse before he or she is even born?"

"Of course not, when you put it that way. But I would protect..."

"Have you been able to protect yourself all these years?"

"Well, I'm not dead yet," Grace said.

"That's just about the saddest summation of a life that I've ever heard," said Janice.

~*~

Grace discussed with Dr. Flanagan the possibility of having Mother committed. Choices were not abundant. There were either nursing homes or mental hospitals.

"You'd go before a judge and convince him to have your mother declared incompetent," Dr. Flanagan said. "That's the only way she can be admitted to a care facility without her consent. Nursing homes could deal with her physical needs, but not her mental health issues; mental hospitals would probably just warehouse her, dose her up and wait for her to die. She's too old for most psychiatrists to consider her a candidate for treatment."

"Either option sounds horrible," Grace said. "You know, she seems calmer lately. Maybe she's just wearing out."

"Some dementia patients do enter a phase of the disease in which they lose their combative spirit and become quite docile. That could be happening with your mother," Dr. Flanagan said doubtfully. "But given her history...Just be careful, Grace."

Mother did seem better, quieter. She was no longer actively sabotaging Grace's daily life. Just being able to pull a blouse out of her closet in the morning and not find all the buttons cut off certainly made Grace's day easier. Mother even put together a couple of simple meals and had them ready when Grace got home from work. She wasn't pleasant, but she wasn't overtly hostile, either. Could it be? Could Mother have moved along in her craziness and reached a more serene place, a place where it wasn't necessary to demonstrate her hatred of Grace? She allowed herself to hope, just a little, as she waited for the Thanksgiving break and Tommy's return.

~*~

Mother never mentioned the possibility of Grace's pregnancy again, and Grace hoped that her foggy mind had failed to retain her suspicions. She herself thought of it every minute. Her lunch times were spent in the library. With growing excitement, she perused baby books, not daring to check them out to take home. Elbows on the table, head bent over the pages, she was completely absorbed. Just think, she was making another human being, a person that would be part of her and Tommy forever. She pored over dry medical texts about the development of tiny fingers and toes, when to expect to feel movement (she savored the phrase "quickening"), and how to calculate her due date. She read about toilet training, and nutritious meals, and temper tantrums in *Dr. Spock's Baby and Childcare*. Some pages she could recite by heart. It was a very private time when the baby was hers alone, before she told even Tommy.

She thought she was carrying a girl. She called her Martha in her mind, after the responsible sister in the Bible. She'd heard Martha's story in Sunday school on one of the few occasions when Mother allowed her to go with Janice. When Jesus came to visit Martha and Mary, Mary sat at his feet, no doubt making moony eyes at him. Martha went out in the kitchen and got a meal together. She was strong, responsible and capable. The way Grace saw it, Martha got things done, and she wasn't intimidated by anyone, not even Jesus.

She was too frightened and too damaged to be a Martha herself, but now she'd been given another chance to get it right, this time with her own child. *I'll teach her to be fearless, to stand up for herself. Martha Rose won't be afraid of anything. She'll love me best in the world - me and her daddy - and we'll always protect her.* In her mind's eye, Grace could see a serious little face looking up at her as the source of all good things. She loved Martha already.

Entering the house quietly one evening after work, she tiptoed into the dim living room hoping to see Mother sleeping in front of the television. The room was shrouded in the shadows of autumn dusk, lit only by the flickering flames of the gas fireplace. She heard a thin thread of sound, and the creak of the rocking chair moving slowly back and forth, back and forth. As her eyes adjusted to the dimness, she saw that Mother was rocking and crooning to a tiny bundle she held in her arms. Grace's scalp prickled as she heard her mother's hoarse voice mumbling a travesty of a lullaby.

Mother looked up, her eyes gleaming in the ambient light, and met Grace's horrified gaze. Deliberately, without breaking eye contact, she unwrapped the tiny figure she held, slowly unwinding the blanket around it. Grace recognized her old baby doll, Susie. Grinning, singing, Mother slowly twisted Susie's head around and around until it came off in her hand. She tossed it into the fire.

CHAPTER TEN

2014

Martha took Lavender out of the house under the cover of a moonless, velvety night. To make it seem less frightening, less like flight, she called herself Jemima Bond, and demanded a martini, shaken not stirred. Hidden under a blanket on the floor of the back seat of Martha's car, Lavender even giggled a time or two at Martha's attempts at the Bond theme song.

"No, you idiot, that's the Batman theme," Lavender said, her voice muffled.

"Batman, Bond, whatever. Don't annoy me or I'll activate the tire spikes."

Beneath her feigned playfulness, Martha kept a wary eye out for Kevin. She saw no lurking figures and no car followed them away from their mother's house. Just to be extra sure, she took a serpentine route to Pat's house, doubling back in several places, and once pausing in a drugstore parking lot, waiting there for a few minutes to see if Kevin showed up. He didn't, and Lavender was wailing about becoming car sick, so Martha proceeded to their destination. Approaching Pat's house, she flashed her brights and the garage door rolled up as she turned into the driveway. She pulled into the garage and waited until Pat pressed the remote control to roll the door back down before she would allow Lavender to emerge from her hiding place. Lavender crawled out and stretched, groaning, as she eased her body back into an upright position.

"You sure took the scenic route," she said reproachfully. "Aunt Pat, are you sure you're up for all this cloak and dagger stuff?"

Pat caught Martha's eye, patted her pocket, winked, and nodded. Uncharacteristically, she said nothing, just took Lavender in a huge hug and ushered her into the house. Inside, all the curtains were tightly drawn and only a few dim lights burned. Martha saw piles of pots and pans stacked in front of the doors. Anybody trying to get in would set off a clatter to rival any burglar alarm.

Pat led the way to the kitchen through the narrow path between her piles of treasures. A feast was laid out on table and counters: meatloaf and cream of broccoli soup, potato salad and chocolate chip cookies, cherry tarts and pimento cheese sandwiches, iced tea and lemonade and a pot of fresh coffee.

"Gosh, Aunt Pat, did you cook all day?" Martha asked.

"You know I cook when I'm nervous, so you may as well enjoy it. Somebody's got to eat all this. Here, Lavender, have one of these tarts. You're too thin, child."

Martha noticed ruefully that, once again, it was Lavender who warranted the fussing and feeding. She helped herself to a tart, anyway. Jemima Bond also needed nourishment.

She left them curled up contentedly in front of the television, watching *The Sound of Music* on the Movie Channel, steadily munching their way through Pat's feast. They barely looked up when she said she was leaving. Good, Martha thought. *The less they think about what I might be doing, the better.* As she closed the door behind her she heard their voices raised in song as they harmonized with Julie Andrews. "Me, a name I call myself. Fa, a long, long way to run."

Martha reflected soberly that she did have a long, long way to run. She drove slowly home. Tomorrow she'd wave goodbye to her family. She'd already laid the groundwork, talking about a week-long out-of-town conference on basket-weaving, one of her hobbies that she simply couldn't miss. The boys were worried only about their food supply. After she listed all the meals packed in the freezer and the snacks in the pantry, they bent their heads back over their mobile devices and tuned her out again. She had no doubt they'd be fine.

Martha's real worry was the dog, Cha-Cha. "She's supposed to be our family dog, but no one takes care of her except me," she said to Zach. "She has to go out every four or five hours, and she likes to nibble all day, so keep her food dish filled. Don't forget to give her fresh water every morning. Look, I'm posting a chart with her schedule here on the refrigerator. Check it every day."

Zach laughed at what he called her Marthatude and promised she'd find Cha-Cha in the pink of health when she returned home. Then, there was nothing else to be done. All in all, she seemed to be quite expendable once the food questions were settled. From her teenage boys she expected nothing else, but she was a little disappointed that Zach didn't mention that he'd miss her. She'd have to think more about that when all this was over. For now, though, she was focused on only one thing: Kevin.

Martha had a plan. In a suitcase hidden under her bed, she'd stashed a black wig, one of Lavender's baseball caps, and an outfit that had belonged to their mother. There was a wooden baseball bat—aluminum wouldn't do for the job she had in mind—and a disposable cell phone in the event she had to make a call she didn't want traced. She wasn't sure why that might be necessary, but she'd seen enough crime shows on television to know it could happen. At the very bottom were an LED flashlight and a can of mace. Just in case the bat didn't work.

The next morning, Martha waited until everyone had left the house. Then she donned the wig, cap and clothing. Surveying herself in the full-length mirror in her bedroom, she thought she could pass for Lavender at a distance. They were about the same size, and her mother's baggy clothing cancelled out shape, anyway. She drove her car to the airport, parked it in the long-term deck, walked to the line of cabs in front of the terminal and climbed into a taxi. In it, she went to her mother's house. There wasn't a soul to be seen on the street when she arrived. Daytimes meant the neighborhood emptied out while everyone was at work. She paid the driver, and scurried inside. She was in place.

Making several trips, Martha carried a thick quilt, a couple of pillows, several books, a flashlight and extra batteries up to the attic. Her shoulder brushing against the wall for balance, she placed her feet carefully as she navigated the narrow steps. On the sheet of plywood nearest the trapdoor, she assembled her supplies. Her weapons. She saw Lavender's provisions nearby. It seemed the sisters were thinking along the same lines, but Martha intended to carry it farther than Lavender could imagine.

Anyone climbing into the attic had to raise both arms, and push up the trapdoor while standing on an eighteen-inch wide step. Martha liked the mental picture of Kevin teetering precariously, arms raised, and vulnerable.

The trap was set. She was ready.

~*~

Nothing happened the first day. Despite displaying herself temptingly as Lavender, working in the yard all afternoon and sitting with the curtains open at night, there was no sign of Kevin. It would be wonderful if he'd simply moved on. That's what she wanted, after all—just that he leave Lavender alone. But Martha admitted to herself that it would be a shame if all her careful planning was wasted. She believed she'd thought of everything, and part of her just wanted to see if it worked. Plus, there was a lot of anger involved. She was furious at Kevin. How dare he hurt her sister and then stalk her! How dare he laugh in Martha's face! Her fingers fairly itched to feel the heft of that baseball bat. She longed to smash that smirk off his face. She slept in the attic that night, but despite waking at every creak and whisper in the eaves, she saw the dawn break uneventfully.

The second day, she decided to speed things along. Patience wasn't her long suit. After all, she couldn't stay here masquerading as Lavender forever. She dialed Kevin's number, let it ring once, and then hung up. She knew he'd see the missed call on his phone's log, and, computer whiz that he was, trace it. The rest of the day passed slowly. Again, she worked in the yard, her scalp prickling with heat under the black wig. Her mother's herbaceous borders never looked better, and Martha developed two blisters on her trowel hand. She slept in the attic again that night, but heard nothing.

In the morning when she opened the front door to get the paper, a long yellow scarf, one of Lavender's, was tied to the doorknob. She made a great show of clutching the scarf and looking around fearfully. Then she went back into the house and stayed there for the rest of the day. Let Kevin think he'd spooked her. He liked his women frightened. She sent thought waves to him: *come and get me, big man. Come and try this sister on for size.*

~*~

It was very late. Having fallen into an uneasy doze in the attic, Martha was roused by the sound of the kitchen door opening stealthily. It had a persistent creak that Tommy never had been able to find and subdue with WD40. She'd locked the door that night, knowing it could be easily opened with a credit card; she'd done it herself when she'd forgotten her key. Now she sat up slowly, every nerve reaching out, listening, listening. Footsteps like a whisper, so quiet she barely heard them, crossed the kitchen, and entered the hall. They went through the house, pausing in each room. Then they returned.

"Laaaavender. Where aaaare you? Laaaavender?"

Her scalp tightened as every hair on her head stood up. The singsong message was coming from the hall directly below her. She held her breath, for a moment as terrified as she knew her sister had been.

Get hold of yourself. You're not Lavender, and you're not afraid of this scumbag. You're ready for him. He can only scare you if you decide to be scared. Deliberately, she moved a bit, making a board beneath her creak.

"Oho! Are you hiding up in the attic, Lavender? You must be, because you aren't anywhere down here. You were a bad girl to take my money and run away. Bad girls need to be punished so they can remember to be good. I'm going to make sure you remember to be a very good girl, Lavender."

The footsteps, no longer quiet, told her of Kevin's ascent up the steps. She heard his body brushing the wall. He'd be there in seconds. Heart pounding, Martha picked up her baseball bat and stood in the crouch that meant a homerun when she was the star of the high school girls' baseball team. She waited.

CHAPTER ELEVEN

1972

Dr. Flanagan listened, head bent over the stethoscope pressed to Mother's chest, but it didn't take a doctor to see that that chest was not rising and falling. He raised his head and shook it: no.

"She's gone, Grace," he said.

She looked back at him, wordless. Their eyes held.

"I'm going to put the cause of death as heart failure," he said. "That's what we all die of, in the end."

"Dr. Flanagan, I—"

"Your mother had serious health problems," Dr. Flanagan's voice cut across Grace's. "She was in congestive heart failure and had frequent attacks of arrhythmia. Since she refused to take her medicine or follow my directions, I can't say that her death was unexpected."

"But I—"

"No, Grace. I'm the one who signs the death certificate and this is my call."

~*~

There were arrangements to be made. The funeral director was summoned, a hearse arrived at the house, and Mother left for the last time.

"It's hard to believe she's really gone," Grace said, standing in the driveway surrounded by concerned neighbors.

"She was a sick woman, I know, but this was sudden, wasn't it, Grace?" asked Mrs. Yoder from next door.

"She said she didn't feel well last night. I thought if she wasn't better this morning, I'd call Dr. Flanagan."

"There, there, Grace. Your mother had a lot of health problems. How were you to know? You're not a medical person. You did your best, I'm sure. You've always done your best." Mrs. Yoder nodded firmly at Grace, her eyes full of the knowledge of what Grace's best had meant over the years.

"We all knew there were...difficulties," she continued. "I blame myself that I didn't help you. I just didn't know what to do. But you've grown up to be a fine girl in spite of everything. I wish you the best now, Grace."

Grace murmured her thanks, and the neighbors took their leave, patting her shoulder, shaking her hand, promising they'd return with casseroles, and if she needed anything, anything at all, just let them know. She went back into the house. It seemed to ring with Mother's absence.

Grace went into Mother's bedroom, the room in which she'd drawn her last breath. The sheets were crusted with vomit. She stripped the bed down to the mattress, bundled all the bedding into a large plastic bag, and stuffed it into the garbage can. In the closet, she swept armloads of clothing off the hanging rods, and into another trash bag. Shoes, the contents of dresser drawers, everything Mother had touched and lived with went into bags. Not all at once, but one by one, those bags would be put out with the trash. She'd wait a few days for decency's sake, then call the Salvation Army and ask them to pick up the bedroom furniture and Mother's recliner. She was determined to purge this house.

When she came to the box of alphabet quilt blocks far back on the closet shelf, something stayed her hand. She looked again at the block with the letter R, and the bloodstains from her pricked finger. That memory wasn't a good one. But the other blocks had been worked by women and girls in her family, a line of stitchers that transcended time. Maybe someday she'd finish the quilt and it would be the only memento of her childhood. Mother had gotten rid of everything else, except for poor old Susie, now headless. But Susie hadn't lost her head in vain. She'd been Mother's graphic early warning.

She walked to the kitchen and put a large pot of water on the stove to boil. The cup, saucer, tea ball and teaspoon from Mother's last herbal tea went into the boiling water. Counter tops were wiped down with bleach. Dishtowels went into a hot water and bleach load in the washer. The smell of chlorine filled the air.

Finally finished, Grace looked out the window over the kitchen sink. Her father's herb and wild flower garden stood fading in the late-autumn sunshine. There'd been a frost and the plants around the perimeter of the bed were dying. The Sweet William and yarrow were brown and drooping, but the monkshood in the center stood tall, its purple blossoms vivid.

Grace donned gardening gloves and went out into the yard. Stooping over the bed, she began methodically pulling the plants out of the ground and throwing them on a bonfire. She saw Mrs. Yoder watching from her kitchen window, so she waved. Mrs. Yoder, taking that as an invitation to satisfy her curiosity, emerged from her house and walked over to where Grace was working.

"Grace, dear, surely that can wait. You don't need to be doing yard work on such a sad day."

"It helps to keep busy," Grace said. "This old garden of my Dad's is so overgrown and scraggly, I can't stand to look at it any longer. I've been meaning to clean it out, and today I need to keep moving. Maybe I'll be able to sleep tonight if I wear myself out."

"Well...you know best, dear. Call me if you need anything." Mrs. Yoder shivered in the chilly wind, pulled her cardigan tight around her shoulders, and went back into her house.

Grace worked on. When the bed was reduced to bare earth, she raked it smooth. Burning herbs sent up fragrant plumes of smoke from the bonfire. She stood looking into the flames.

"Thank you, Daddy," she whispered.

~*~

"Tommy, I have something to tell you. It's important."

Tommy came home from college a few days early for Thanksgiving break when he heard the news of Grace's mother's death. For the first time, he was able to enter Grace's home. They sat entwined on the sofa, feeling like they were in the wrong house, both liberated and ill at ease.

"Sure, hon, what is it?"

"I'm not sure how you're going to feel about this. It's unexpected, not something we'd planned. Maybe you won't be happy." Grace looked into Tommy's face anxiously.

"Well, spit it out. It can't be all that bad."

"Okay. Um…The thing is, you see, well, I'm pregnant."

Tommy's mouth fell open. "You're going to have a baby?"

"That's what pregnant means," Grace said.

"But how did that happen?"

"The usual way, Tommy. You were there, remember?"

"I'm sounding like an idiot." Tommy made a visible effort to pull himself together. "We've talked about having kids. It's something we both want, just a little early. And now that your mother's gone, she won't be standing in our way anymore."

"Tommy, I need to tell you something about Mother's death."

"Let's talk about that later, sweetheart. Right now, I want to get my mind around the fact that I'm going to be a father. Holy cow! I'm going to be a father!" He laughed delightedly.

"I think it's a girl," Grace said, "I just have a feeling. And if it is, I want to name her Martha Rose. Do you like that name?"

"It's beautiful. And if it's a boy, Thomas Allen McGuire, Junior. We'll get married right away, and you can come back to school with me after the break, or if not now, after Christmas break. I'll get another part-time job. We'll figure it out."

"I've got to wait until Mother's estate is settled," Grace said. "She didn't have a will. I guess her thinking was too disorganized to allow for that kind of planning. I'll inherit everything, eventually, as her only next of kin. It's ironic. I'm sure she'd rather have left it to an old cat's home than for me to get a red cent."

"Maybe not. She was a sick woman, Grace, and not only physically. Who knows, maybe she loved you after all, down deep, in her own weird way. Maybe she was just so mentally ill that she couldn't show it."

"Don't say that, Tommy! Don't say she loved me."

Tommy looked at Grace's horrified face in alarm. "Okay, okay. Simmer down, I won't say it again."

CHAPTER TWELVE

2014

"Dammit!" Martha cursed under her breath when light flooded the attic. She'd forgotten about the switch at the top of the steps that turned on the bare overhead bulb in the rafters. The element of surprise in the dark that she'd been counting on was lost.

"I can see better to hit him, though," she told herself, watching the trapdoor like a cat watches a mouse hole. She heard the steps creak under Kevin's weight. He was still sing-songing: "Laaaavender. Coming to get you, Laaaavender."

Suddenly the trapdoor flew up and to one side, and there he was. His arms were raised, his head and shoulders already in the attic. Because she stood behind him, he didn't see her for an instant. It was her perfect shot. She tensed her arms to swing the bat. But she couldn't.

The realization that the *thunk* she already heard in her mind's ear would be her bat connecting with a living skull held her frozen. Martha could swat flies; she could crush spiders. What she couldn't do was remove a mouse from a trap or pick up a dead chipmunk from the lawn. There was something about the squishiness of the soft little bodies that turned her guts to jelly. Now here was a man's head—a man she despised, but still a human being made of vulnerable soft tissue—and she couldn't smash her bat into his head. She just couldn't.

As she stood in horrified realization that her best-laid plans had failed to take into account her own weakness, Kevin swiveled his head and shoulders toward her. When he saw her in the black wig, his jaw dropped.

"What the hell? Martha?"

She stared at him, unable to speak, and unable to lower the bat.

"Playing a little dress-up? I thought I was coming after Lavender, but you'll do, Martha. You'll do." Kevin was taunting her, just as he'd done when she confronted him at his house. "I've been wanting to take you down a peg or two, you self-righteous bitch."

He braced his hands on the attic floor, readying himself to vault upward, and his movement released her. Dropping her bat, she pushed his shoulders with both hands. His face reflected first surprise, then fear as he scrambled to keep his footing. Martha heard the clatter of his shoes losing purchase on the stairs. Then he was gone, except for his hands, which clutched the sides of the trapdoor opening. He was dangling by his fingers, suspended over the front of the bookshelf. It wasn't much of a drop. He could easily let go and land on his feet without injury. Closing her eyes, and holding her breath, Martha stepped on his fingers with her full weight. Kevin struggled to free his hands. His yell of pain was cut short by a crash as he fell, his head bouncing off the shelves on the way down. Then it was quiet.

She looked through the opening, but the light in the attic rendered the hallway below dark as a pocket. Picking up her flashlight, she trained it down to where Kevin's body sprawled. His eyes, half-open, seemed to be peering up at her. Blood pooled under his head. One leg turned out from the hip at an unnatural angle. She couldn't tell if he was breathing. Martha sat down suddenly, one hand clutching her head, the other her stomach.

"Holy crap," she said aloud. "What do I do now?"

~*~

Lavender and Pat decided to use their enforced solitude to work on the quilt blocks. "We can finish if we keep at it," Pat said. "Once we get the blocks embroidered, we'll take them to Tiny Stitches, that quilting shop on Oak Street. They have people there who can help us mark the quilting pattern, attach the batting and backing, and then quilt it on that big machine."

"You mean we aren't going to quilt it by hand?" Lavender asked, disappointment in her voice.

"Quilting's pretty hard for beginners like us. And we don't have a frame. You have to stretch the fabric tight to stitch it, and your fingers get pricked. One of the women at the shop said she has to stop when her fingers bleed."

"I wonder if that's what happened to the block with the letter R," Lavender said. "It looks like it's been bled on."

"No telling. I say let's just get this old thing finished, once and for all. If that means machine quilting, that's fine by me. It will be done and usable," Pat said. "And remind me to soak that R block in cold water before we add it to the quilt."

They cross-stitched companionably, stopping for cups of tea and yoga poses. "Aunt Pat, you're still really limber," Lavender said, as Pat hoisted her ample rear toward the ceiling in Downward Facing Dog. A small silver pistol fell from her pocket onto the floor.

"Hey! What are you doing with a gun?" Lavender asked.

"Oh, never you mind. It's just something I got for protection. I'm only carrying it out of an abundance of caution."

"But do you think K-Kevin will come here?"

"Of course not. He doesn't know I exist, and Martha was careful that no one was following her when she brought you. You weren't visible in the car, anyway, remember?"

"What do you think Martha is up to? She was so secretive about it," Lavender said. "Said she'd only tell me what I needed to know, and all I needed to know was that I'd be staying with you for a few days."

"Wouldn't tell me anything, either," Pat said. "But knowing Martha, she has a plan. Never saw such a one for planning."

"But do you think she's safe? K-Kevin can be really mean, and he's strong." Lavender rubbed her ribs reminiscently. There was still a sore spot.

"Lord, child, I hope she's not doing anything to put herself in danger. We're forbidden to call her or to leave this house." Pat paused thoughtfully. "But she's not here to make us mind, is she?"

Lavender looked scared. "I don't think we should d-disobey Martha," she said. "Let's give her a little more t-time."

"Don't you get all worked up and stressed, honey, it just makes you stutter. We'll wait right here until we hear from her."

~*~

When the phone rang at two in the morning, Pat, who hadn't closed her eyes, pounced on it. "Hello?"

"Aunt Pat, it's Martha."

"Martha! What's going on? Why are you calling? What's wrong?"

"I need help. I don't know what to do. He's just lying there on the floor and he's so still. Maybe I've killed him."

Pat heard the rising hysteria in Martha's voice. "Calm, calm, Martha. Take a breath. Tell me where you are."

"I'm at Mom's."

"And who's lying on the floor?"

"Kevin. I pushed him and stepped on his hands, and he fell out of the attic, and there's blood."

"Martha. Are you safe?"

"I guess so. He's unconscious, or maybe dead, I don't know."

"Did you call 911?"

"I can't! What if they arrest me? Think of my kids and Zach. I can't go to jail, Aunt Pat, I just can't."

"But didn't he break into the house?"

"He'll say I lured him in and then assaulted him."

"Okay. We can talk about that later. Listen to me: stay put, we're on our way. But if Kevin starts to come to, you get out of that house, into your car and leave. Do you understand me, Martha?"

"Get in my car and leave," Martha repeated. She was too distraught to remember her car was at the airport.

"We'll be right there."

Pat shook Lavender awake with some difficulty. Fear didn't seem to affect her sleep. "Wake up, Lavender, wake up. Martha needs us."

Her sister's name finally penetrated Lavender's sleep-fogged mind, and she sat up in bed. "What's wrong? Where is she?"

"We have to go to your Mom's house. Martha said Kevin is there, and she's hurt him. She doesn't know what to do."

"K-Kevin is there?" Lavender clutched the sheet to her chin.

"Get up. We're going to help Martha." Pat's tone of voice brooked no arguments.

Lavender scrambled into her clothes and into Pat's car. Pat always said she couldn't see to drive at night, but she was driving rapidly through the darkness now. She killed the car's headlights before they pulled into the driveway and reached up to switch off the interior dome light.

"Don't slam the door," she whispered to Lavender. "We don't want to wake the neighbors."

Quietly, they entered the dark house. Martha was waiting for them by the door.

"He's still just lying there," she whispered, clutching at them as they entered.

"Have you checked to see if he has a pulse?" Pat asked in a normal tone of voice. After all, there was no need to whisper inside.

"No. I can't bear to touch him," Martha said. Panicked and shaking, she kept a death grip on Lavender's hand. For the second time in her life – and both in the past hour – she couldn't bring herself to act.

Lavender squared her shoulders and disengaged Martha's hand. "I'll check," she said, to astonished gazes from Martha and Pat. She walked into the hall where Kevin lay. Gingerly, she placed two fingers on his neck.

"Yep, still has a heartbeat," she called back to the other two, who looked at each other in amazement.

"But we need to tie him up before he comes around," Lavender continued. "Where are those zip-ties Dad used to have?"

"I think I saw some in the garage," Martha said.

"Well, go get me a couple," Lavender said, and Martha did.

Together, the women crossed Kevin's arms over his body, and fastened his hands tightly together.

"I don't think we'll have to tie his feet," Lavender said. "He's not walking anywhere on that leg."

The women surveyed the twisted leg. "Looks like his hip is out of joint," Pat said. "I put many a limb back in its socket when I was an Army nurse. Bet I could pop this one back, too." Pat bent to pick up Kevin's leg, but Lavender stopped her.

"Let's leave it for now, Aunt Pat. We really don't want him to be able to walk."

Pat glanced at Martha, whose face was white with shock.

"Lavender, go put the kettle on, and get out the teabags and sugar," she said. "Your sister needs a cup of hot, sweet tea."

The women left Kevin where he lay and sat at the kitchen table. When Martha had started on her second cup of tea and had some color back in her face, Pat could restrain herself no longer.

"Martha, what were you thinking? You always have a plan, and obviously this outcome was not part of it. What did you think would happen?"

"I was disguised as Lavender," Martha said. "I waited in the dark attic and planned to take him by surprise--give him some good whacks with my bat so he'd know what it feels like to be hurt. He's a bully. I thought if he believed Lavender was finally standing up to him, he'd back off, leave her alone."

"And what went wrong?"

"He turned the light on from the hall switch, and when he got up there, he looked right at me. I couldn't hit him," Martha confessed. "But then he came after me, and I panicked, and pushed him and he fell and now he's really hurt, and that wasn't the plan and I don't know what to do." Her voice rose in a wail on the last words.

There was silence in the kitchen, until Lavender spoke.

"I know what we should do."

"*You* know, honey?" Pat asked. "*You* know what to do with the man who stalked you, and beat you, and now is lying unconscious on the hallway floor?"

Lavender rose and paced the few steps the small space allowed.

"Here's what I think," she said, and began ticking off ideas on her fingers. "We can't call the police, we've already established that we don't need the trouble that would cause. We can't take him to the hospital, he'd rat us out immediately. While it would be tempting to just put him in the car and push him out beside the road somewhere, I know none of us is capable of that. So what's left?"

Pat and Martha looked at her blankly.

"We have to keep him," Lavender said.

CHAPTER THIRTEEN

1978

Grace held Martha's hand and carried Lavender. The girls were worn out from their afternoon in the park. Lavender was asleep, her cheek pillowed on Grace's shoulder, while Martha dragged heavily on her mother's arm.

Arriving at the house, Grace took a moment to admire it, despite the burden of her sleepy children. She and Tom had bought it with the money from her mother's estate - her father's insurance money finally came to her after all. The original farm house was part of acreage that had been subdivided for suburban McMansions. It stood on a little island of lawn among the fancy houses all around it. Austere in its simplicity, the house had twelve foot ceilings, quarter-sawn hardwood floors and shiplap walls. The kitchen was outdated, the plumbing made strange noises and the old boiler in the basement had a mind of its own. But they'd painted and sanded and pressure-washed, wall-papered and polished, putting their hands and hearts and sweat into every room until it became precious to them.

Grace slid Lavender into her crib and covered her, tiptoeing from the room. Martha had dropped onto the sofa and fallen asleep, so she tucked the Afghan around her and left her there. Her nap, at age five, wouldn't be a long one, but with any luck Lavender might sleep for a couple of hours. Grace would have time to make a nice dinner. She glanced at the clock. Tommy would be home in three hours time enough to put a pot roast in the oven, his favorite. She got busy in the kitchen.

Good smells of roasting meat and vegetables greeted Tommy at the door. The girls, rested, bathed, and wearing matching pajamas, ran to greet him. He swung Martha up on his shoulders and carried little Lavender, upside down and squealing, into the kitchen.

"Honey, I'm home," he said unnecessarily, kissing Grace on the cheek.

"Yeah, you sure are," Grace said, laughing. "You'll have these girls so riled up we'll never get them settled."

Her eyes were filled with love as she looked at her husband and daughters. Warm and secure, loved and cared for, her girls' childhoods could not have been more different than hers.

This is how I make it up. This is how I atone. I'll never be sorry for keeping them safe.

It wasn't automatic. She admitted that to herself. She had no motherly role model on which to pattern herself. Days when the girls were difficult—cutting teeth, testing boundaries, being naughty—she sometimes had to consult her feelings and then do the opposite. So undelivered slaps became hugs, and screams became whispers before they ever left her mouth. Did it make her seem buttoned up, wound too tight? The girls didn't seem to notice. They were healthy, happy and thriving. With every year in her own home with her own family, it became easier to be the Grace she wanted to be.

She never talked about the past and became skilled in diverting conversations that went there. Most people, she knew, really preferred to talk about themselves anyway, so a well-put question—where did you go to school? What was your favorite thing to do with your parents? How did your mother wake you in the mornings?—were a sure-fire detour away from her life. As a result, she got the reputation of being a good conversationalist and a caring person.

And she *was* a caring person. She cared for her children, her husband, her home, her garden, her car. When Martha started preschool, Grace volunteered to be a room mother, never failing to show up with Halloween decorations, Christmas cookies and Easter eggs. Tommy had the whitest shirts and shiniest shoes in his office. When he protested that he could shine his own shoes, she told him truthfully that she loved doing it for him.

Aside from the constant self-monitoring to make sure she wasn't like her mother, Grace was happy. If it just weren't for the nightmares.

"Honey, honey, wake up," Tommy would mumble, stroking her hair away from her wet brow. "Another bad dream. It's okay, you're here with me."

"Mother..."

"I know. But she's gone, remember. Go back to sleep now."

Eventually, she would sleep again, warmed by Tommy's solid body at her side. Maybe someday the dreams would stop.

There was an article about psychiatric counseling in *Good Housekeeping*, and it struck a chord within her because she longed for the relief of telling someone the whole story. Maybe it would be healing to just sit down and unload the whole thing as honestly as possible to an impartial person who would keep her confidence. She even went so far as to call a psychiatrist's office and inquire about the cost. Thirty dollars an hour! It would be a major hit to the household budget, and Grace didn't have money of her own. Mother's estate had paid for their house; there was nothing left over. The nearest doctor was a half-hour's drive away, which meant she'd have to take Tommy to work and find a sitter for the girls, disrupting everyone's day. And what would Tommy think? Maybe that she was crazy, like her mother. Better to suffer the nightmares, to carry the knowledge inside her and never let it out. She'd made a choice. Now she'd live with it.

~*~

The years passed happily. Martha and Lavender grew long-legged as colts, lost their baby teeth, and navigated multiplication tables. Grace would have been completely content except for one worry.

Lavender was just too pretty. No, she was beautiful. Every boy who saw her wanted to take her out, and she wasn't old enough—only fourteen. Grace had seen older boys, even grown men, eyeing Lavender in the street. It scared her to death. She tried to talk to Lavender about it.

"Honey, you know you have to be really careful around boys," she said. In her head she heard her mother's voice: "Slut! Whore!" *Careful, careful. Do the opposite.*

"Oh, Mom, don't worry. I know how to take care of myself," Lavender said dreamily. She was dreamy a lot these days.

"Yeah, right," Martha said. "And if you forget, I'll be right there watching you."

At eighteen, Martha was a lofty high school senior keeping a beady eye on her freshman sister. What she saw worried her, but she didn't freak her mother out by reporting the times she'd caught Lavender kissing some pimply kid behind the bleachers, or necking in the back row of the movies, or responding to wolf whistles with flirtatious smiles. Parents, especially mothers, were fragile. Some things they were better off not knowing. Martha renewed her vigilance. She worried about next year, when she was away at college. Who would watch out for Lavender then?

But despite Martha's worries, Lavender made it through high school without major mishaps. She was homecoming queen, a cheerleader, and dated every Friday and Saturday night. Martha, meanwhile, bent over her books in the library study carrel. She intended to be a high school English teacher, and every course she took was aimed straight at that goal. No easy A's, no pop culture cake-walk classes for her. She got her teaching degree, easily passed the accreditation test, and went to work in the high school she'd graduated from only four years previously.

No one knew what Lavender meant to do after she finished high school. Tommy and Grace hoped she'd follow Martha to college, although Lavender showed little aptitude for studies.

"Maybe she needs a gap year," Grace said. "Maybe she should get a little job and grow up a bit."

But Lavender surprised everyone by announcing that she was going to New York to pursue a modeling career.

"You don't know how to be a model," Grace said, stating an obvious truth.

"No girl of mine is going to be on her own in New York City," thundered her usually mild-mannered father.

"Get real," snorted Martha. "You'll get mugged the first night."

But Lavender's languid, passive-aggressive ways could hide a will of steel and she would not be deterred. Tommy and Grace discussed, pleaded, threatened and begged, but in the end, Lavender prevailed.

"She'll be safe if you look after her," Grace said to Martha. "Please, I know it's asking too much, but please, honey, would you go with her? For your little sister? For our peace of mind?"

It was a plea Martha'd been hearing all her life and she could no more resist it than a fire horse could ignore clanging bells. She left her new teaching job and moved to the big city to look after her little sister yet again.

Of course, Lavender got exactly what she wanted. She walked into the Ford Modeling Agency with no appointment and asked to see Eileen Ford herself. The receptionist had been there long enough to know that lilac eyes, long legs and jet-black hair warranted a quick call to her boss, and in a very few minutes, Lavender was ushered into the inner sanctum.

Predictably enough, the camera loved her. Never a super-model—that would have taken much more effort than Lavender was prepared to expend—she didn't lack for jobs, mostly print ads and catalog work. She was beautiful and agreeable, showed up on time, didn't mind changing her clothes a hundred times, and smilingly refused the lines of cocaine sketched on hand mirrors. Her success may have been limited, but it was exactly in line with her ambitions.

Martha handled the mundane aspects of their lives. She found a tiny apartment and made it homey. Shopped for groceries and cooked the small meals that Lavender would consent to eat. Landed a teaching job in an inner-city school. For the rest of her life, she treasured that experience, so different than anything her suburban upbringing had afforded her. It was there that she met another idealistic young teacher, Zach Rendell, the man who became her husband. Life in New York gradually took on a comfortable rhythm under Martha's excellent organizational skills.

Then, suddenly, Lavender was done with modeling. There was a man, of course, and he didn't want his girlfriend parading herself in front of everyone. He was persistent, she was passive, and so he prevailed. They sequestered themselves in his beach house and spent an idyllic summer.

Then that was over, too, and Lavender was ready to move back home for a while. Martha followed dutifully, resumed her teaching job at the local high school, and married Zach, who followed her home from New York.

"A happy ending, don't you think, honey?" Grace asked hopefully.

"Yeah, I guess," Martha responded. She didn't voice her resentment at the assumption that her life should take second place to Lavender's. What was the point?

Martha had her husband, and, in due time, her two sons. Life was structured and orderly. Lavender had a succession of men, a string of adventures, periodic break-ups, and a lot of financial scrapes. She floated above it all, unengaged on a meaningful level, always grateful to be rescued, never learning from experience. After all, her big sister was there when needed, solid and dependable, ready to spring into action.

Grace knew she'd set the wheels in motion from the very beginning of her daughters' lives. She'd succeeded in raising a fearless, capable woman, a Martha, who could handle anything life threw at her. She'd failed with Lavender. Lavender was just special, different. She had her grandmother's eyes and sometimes their gaze made Grace shudder with memories. It was important to keep Lavender safe from frustration and failure, so that her eyes would never flash with the awful anger Grace remembered too well. She and Tom wouldn't be around forever, so there was nothing else to do but make sure Martha understood she could never stop taking care of Lavender.

Their mother's indoctrination continued to reach long fingers into the daughters' lives from beyond the grave, until the night Kevin lay broken in the hall. After that, everything changed.

CHAPTER FOURTEEN

2014

Together, the women lifted Kevin under the arms and dragged him to the nearest bedroom. That happened to be Lavender's old room, unchanged since she'd last lived in it as a teenager. The ruffled blue curtains and bedspread, shag carpet and hydrangea print wallpaper didn't accept the addition of a bleeding, unconscious man cheerfully. If rooms could be said to recoil, this one did.

All their strength combined was needed to hoist Kevin's dead weight up onto the bed. Martha hurried to put a towel under his head, which was still seeping blood from a mean-looking cut. Pat leaned over to inspect it.

"Head cuts always bleed like crazy," she said. "Doesn't actually look too bad. I might stick a couple of butterfly bandages over it to pull the edges together. Got any?"

Martha and Lavender smiled. They'd always made fun of their mother for what they called her Band-Aid fetish.

"If there's one thing Mom kept in stock, it's Band-Aids," Martha said. "All kinds, all sizes, all shapes. There's a special shelf in the medicine cabinet for them. I'll get them."

"Lavender, you get me a basin of warm water, scissors, antibiotic ointment, a washcloth and towel. I'll tend to this head wound."

Kevin stirred just then, and moaned. They'd need to hurry before he woke up. Pat washed his scalp, gently snipping the hair away from the cut. He'd have a bald spot, but that was the least of his worries, she thought. Once the wound was dressed, she stood over him, looking thoughtfully at his leg, sticking out at an odd angle from his hip.

"Gonna hurt like hell when he wakes up," she murmured to herself. "Might as well take care of it now, while he's out. The Stimson Maneuver ought to do it. Girls, come here. We're going to put this varmint's hip back into the socket."

"Do you know how?" Martha asked.

"Uh, what did I do for twenty-five years as an Army nurse? I've popped more dislocated joints back into place than your mother had Band-Aids. Now come here and help me turn him over onto his stomach. Lavender, you take hold of his head, right there at his ears, and hold him still. Martha, put both hands on his back, right at the sacrum, and push down. Don't let him flop around. Ready?"

Before they could answer, Pat grabbed Kevin's feet and swung his legs over the edge of the bed. He groaned. Lavender and Martha scrambled to get into position. Then Pat bent his knee and pushed, rotating his leg gently as she did so. There was a click as the femur fit neatly back into the socket. Kevin roared.

They all jumped back, startled by his sudden return to consciousness. His eyes open, but wild and unseeing, he thrashed frantically, struggling to free his bound hands. It lasted a few seconds, and then unconsciousness mercifully descended again.

"Huh," Pat said. "Still got some fight in him. Let's tie his ankles together. I don't want him popping that hip out again."

Lavender reached into a bureau drawer, and brought forth a long, silk scarf. She pulled off Kevin's loafers and matter-of-factly wound the scarf around his ankles until his legs were immobilized.

"You're full of surprises tonight," Pat said. "I keep forgetting that people surprise us, and we surprise ourselves. Hey, are you girls hungry? I sure am."

"What about...?"

"He's not going any place, is he?"

The women sat at the kitchen table, eating raisin bran out of brightly colored Fiesta Ware bowls.

"I feel like I'm about two feet to the left of my body," Martha said. "Like I'm in one of those old *Twilight Zone* episodes when Rod Serling would say, 'You are traveling through another dimension.' This can't be real life."

"I know what you mean," Pat said. "You're the one who always copes, but you're in a panic. Lavender is usually off somewhere in left field, but she's calm and capable. I snapped straight back from has-been retiree into Army nurse. I don't even recognize us."

She was interrupted by a bellow from Lavender's old bedroom. Kevin was awake. The women trooped back into the room, where they found an obviously disoriented captive.

"Wha' the hell?" Kevin said. "Where'm I?"

But before anyone could answer, his eyes closed again. They surveyed him-- mouth agape, drool dribbling down his chin--and shook their heads.

"How could I have ever...?" Lavender said quietly.

But Pat heard. "Now, let's be fair," she said. "None of us look our best after a head injury. I'm sure he's a presentable man when he's whole."

"He's a *whole* lot of trouble, that's for sure," Martha said. "The question is, what are we going to do with him?"

"We're going to take care of him," Pat said, "and then, when he's better, we'll—we'll figure something out."

Kevin's eyes fluttered open again, and this time he looked straight at Lavender.

"Who're *you*?" he asked.

~*~

"We've gone from *Twilight Zone* to that Kathy Bates movie," Martha asked. "The one where she holds a famous writer captive and tortures him."

The women had been up for twenty-four hours straight, caring for Kevin. He was disoriented and loud, demanding to know where he was, who they were and why his hands and legs were bound. They were afraid his voice would carry outside the house, so at least one of them had to be nearby to quiet him whenever he woke.

Pat decreed that Kevin needed fluids, so they pushed frequent sips of water. That led, inevitably, to his shouted demand: "I gotta pee!" He adamantly refused the urinal they offered, and demanded to be taken to the bathroom. Untying his legs and supporting him to, during and from this activity was so difficult and ridiculous that all three women were weak with laughter by the time they dumped him back onto the bed. He regarded them owlishly and asked what was so damn funny.

As Kevin became more wakeful, his demands increased: more pillows, fewer blankets, lower the window shade, turn on the overhead fan, another blanket over his feet, just so. Then there was the constant need for fresh ice packs and keeping track of the rotation of ice on and off his hip joint. When one of the bags sprang a leak, they had to change all the bedding, rolling Kevin from side to side as they eased the wet bottom sheet off and the dry sheet on, a feat which tested even Pat's nursing skills. They were exhausted.

"We should have just finished him off," Lavender said wearily. "It would have been less trouble to dig a grave in the back yard."

Kevin continued to ask who they were, who *she* was, and where he was. The blow to his head had apparently erased his memory.

"That's probably just temporary," Pat said. "Happens with head trauma sometimes. He'll remember eventually. Or he could be faking it. Hard to tell."

Lavender wondered how long it would be before his boss missed him and called the police. His car was nowhere to be found in the immediate neighborhood, so presumably he'd parked it farther away and walked to the house. Wherever it was, someone was sure to wonder about a strange car that seemed to be abandoned. All roads seemed to lead to the police, and those were the very roads she didn't want to travel. She walked in increasing circles until she found Kevin's car, parked three blocks away, the keys still in the ignition. Weak with relief, she drove it to his house and left it in the garage.

Lavender had felt completely justified in taking Kevin's money to escape from him, but she wasn't sure she could convince the authorities of that. Her bruises had long faded. She'd not filed a complaint at the time, nor when Kevin was stalking her, so it would be a he said/she said case. Who would be more believable? A mistress who'd just lost her meal ticket, or a gainfully employed computer expert who owned his own home? No, she couldn't risk police involvement. And now Kevin could file assault charges against Martha. Again, it would be his word against hers as to what really happened in the attic that night. She could hear him now: "I was just checking on a friend. I'd gotten a hang-up call earlier in the day that made me worry about her. The door was unlocked, and I heard a strange noise in the attic. When I went up to see about it, this woman attacked me." And he had the injuries to prove it. Lavender didn't think she could bear it if Martha was hauled off to jail because she'd tried to help.

Martha, meanwhile, knew the clock was ticking. Her bogus basket-weaving weekend was over, and she'd called her husband to say she was staying a couple of extra days to catch up with old friends. She was both grateful and resentful when he accepted the news calmly with no questions. *I could be having a red-hot affair, and he wouldn't even notice.* Yeah, she was going to have to do something about his indifference when all this was over. But now even those extra days were up, and she had to return home.

"Will you be able to manage? I'll come back tomorrow when everyone at my house has gone about their day, but you and Lavender will be here by yourselves all night," she said to Pat.

"No offense, darlin', but you may not have noticed that Lavender and I have been coping just fine."

"You're right, of course. I haven't been much help, have I? I don't know what's come over me."

"Humanity has come over you, Martha. You're not Superwoman, after all." Pat was smiling, and Martha had to smile, too.

"It's kind of a relief, actually," Martha confessed. "I've always felt that I had to rise to any occasion and that I could, if I just made a big enough effort. Well, I couldn't handle this one. If you and Lavender hadn't come to my rescue, I don't know what I would have done."

"I hope we'll always be able to rescue each other; we're family," Pat said gruffly. "Now, you go on home and act like butter wouldn't melt in your mouth. We'll see you tomorrow. Call before you come, because I'll need you to stop at the drugstore and get a cane, and probably some other stuff when I've had time to think about it. If Kevin's going to walk without a limp, I've got to start rehab."

~*~

Lavender called Kevin's boss and said that he'd been called out of town for a death in the family and would be gone for a couple of weeks. She purposely left the time frame vague because none of them, not even Pat, had an accurate idea of how long he'd be laid up. Now that he was becoming increasingly mobile, the memory loss was the most worrisome problem. Under Pat's stern tutelage, he'd graduated from sitting up in a chair to standing to walking gingerly with a cane. It had been a week, and it was time for all of them to go home. But Kevin had no idea where home was.

"His memory will come back," Pat kept insisting. "It almost always does."

But so far, it hadn't.

"Who're you, again?" he asked Lavender for the fiftieth time.

"Lavender. We were...friends."

He could remember Pat's name and Martha's name, but he had to ask Lavender every day. Pat was his favorite. It was Pat he called if he needed to get up during the night. Only she was allowed to help him with his shower or assist him to rise from a chair.

On this afternoon, everyone left the house except Lavender. Pat said she needed fresh air and went for a walk. Martha had to pick up one of her kids from band practice. When Lavender checked on Kevin he was dozing, so she curled up on the sofa with a book and soon she was nodding, too. His voice made her jump.

"Lavender."

"You remember my name. That's something new. Coming."

"Lavender."

She got up, and walked to the bedroom door. Kevin was sitting up in bed. In his hand was a pistol aimed at her head.

"Wh-where did you g-get that?"

"Your Aunt Pat needs to be more careful with her firearms," Kevin said. "It fell out of her pocket when she bent over to get my slippers. Bet she still doesn't know it's gone."

He clicked off the safety, his hand never wavering. Lavender pictured a hot red dot on her forehead.

She turned and ran. Down the hall, through the door, across the front lawn, heels pounding, heart keeping time, she ran. Not until the house was out of sight did she cease to feel the itchy spot between her shoulder blades where a bullet would go. Concentrating hard, she willed her heaving stomach to be still.

In the distance, she saw a familiar figure—Pat,

returning from her walk. Thank God! She hurried to meet her.

"Pat, Kevin's got your g-gun. He p-pointed it at me. I think he would have k-killed me."

"Why, that little turd! He must have slipped it out of my pocket when I was taking care of him. What an ungrateful bastard."

"Well, to be f-fair, my sister did c-cause his injuries."

"And would that have happened if he hadn't been stalking you? If he hadn't punched you? No way, his problems are nobody's fault but his own. What did you do when he aimed the gun at you?"

"I ran," Lavender said. "I'm ashamed to s-say it."

"Don't be. Nobody ever faced down a bullet. We need to know what he's up to now. Let's not go into the house until we've taken a good look around."

Their steps carried them back home as they talked, but when they neared the house they slipped along the hedge that separated the backyard from neighbors. Pat dropped to a crouch that made Lavender grin as she followed suit. The women peeked through the kitchen window—the room was empty. Scuttling along the wall, they surveyed the living and dining rooms through the French doors—empty. Standing on tiptoes, they raised their eyes just above the sill of the room they now thought of as Kevin's. It was empty, too. They went inside and searched the house, ending up in Kevin's room. Pat's gun lay on the pillow like a malignant mint, but Kevin was gone.

CHAPTER FIFTEEN

2014

They made some discreet inquiries, but Kevin hadn't surfaced at his house or job. Eventually, they all went on with their lives. What else was there to do? There were no sightings around town, no phone calls nor offerings on the doorstep. He seemed to have fallen off the planet.

Martha resumed her busy schedule, but kept one nervous eye peeled at all times. Her family commented on her new jumpiness. Pat and Lavender finished the alphabet quilt. There was still a bit of rusty stain on the R block, but Lavender thought it added to the character of the piece. She draped it over the back of the sofa, resolved that it would never again languish unseen in storage.

"It's our history," she said to Martha.

Somehow, it seemed to close a circle she hadn't been aware was open. Seeing it every day, she began to feel an urge to move on. For the first time, there wasn't a man standing by to tell her how.

"What do *you* want to do?" Martha asked, impatience

edging her voice.

"I don't know," Lavender said, "I can't think of anything, really. I guess I'll just keep on living here, if you don't mind."

"I don't mind you living here while the house is on the market. We want it to show well, and an empty house deteriorates quickly. I doubt very much it will sell this late in the summer, but just keep in mind, if it does, you'll have to scoot. But aren't you bored, hanging around Mom's house? It'll be winter soon, and then you'll be stuck inside."

That was a sobering thought. Winters were long, gray and depressing. The house began to feel less like a refuge and more like a prison. She dreamed about her mother one night.

"It was her, and yet it wasn't," she told Martha. "She was a little girl, but still...I knew it was Mom somehow."

"Yeah, okay," Martha said. She was uninterested in dreams. Her own made no sense, and she'd long ago dismissed them as random firings of her brain at rest. Lavender continued.

"The strangest thing was she was lecturing me, this little girl who was my mother. She said I was lazy, and it was her fault. The quilt was in my dream, too, and the little girl was working on it. I told her, I said, 'Mom, we finished the quilt.' What do you suppose it means?"

Martha, seizing the opportunity, said, "I think it means you need to get on with your life. If Mom were here in person, that's what she'd say."

Lavender looked doubtful. In her experience, her mother was more apt to sympathize warmly with whatever problems she had, make her a cup of tea, and offer to write a check. Still, maybe Martha was right. Lavender turned to Aunt Pat for advice.

"Why don't you try some volunteer work?" Pat said. "No commitment, just experiment with different things, and see if you find something that speaks to you."

When she saw an article in the newspaper about the End Domestic Violence Initiative, Lavender remembered those words. Newly formed under the auspices of the YWCA, the program was seeking community volunteers to staff the safe house informally known as the Nest, work in the office, and help with fund-raising. Lavender called, went in for an interview, was accepted, trained, and put to work. Because she was single and didn't have the constraints of a day job, she was asked to spend several nights a week as a kind of house-mother in the Nest. To her own surprise, she loved it. She loved the cloak and dagger secrecy of getting to the house's location. She loved the revolving cast of residents. She loved the late-night conversations with women too worried to sleep, who found a moment's respite by sharing their dreams and fears.

Most of all, she loved the kids. Scrappy, scared, naughty, confused, the children never took their eyes off of their mothers. Unless Lavender was around. Then they gathered at her side, little girls wanting to brush her long, black hair, little boys looking at her with shy, shining eyes. In the company of children for the first time in her adult life, Lavender discovered they filled a place in her heart she hadn't known was empty.

~*~

It was late and the house slept. Lavender sat quietly reading a paperback.

"Miss Lavender?"

A tiny girl stood, trailing her blanket, just outside the circle of lamplight. Her mother had arrived earlier that night holding this little girl's hand, squinting through her almost-closed black eye. Lavender had helped them get settled.

"Yes, Kaylie?"

"Will you hold me? Mama's asleep. I'm scared."

"Of course. Come on."

Lavender pulled Kaylie into her lap. The little girl rubbed the satin binding of her blanket against her cheek and popped her thumb into her mouth. They sat in silence for a few minutes. Then Kaylie removed her thumb and spoke.

"Daddy hit Mama's eye," she said. "And I was crying, and Mama was crying."

"It must have been pretty scary."

"I was very scared. Then policemans came and knocked real hard on the door, and yelled 'Open up, police.' Daddy had to go with them in their car. Then we came here in the dark." Kaylie sighed from her toes.

"You're safe now," Lavender said, resting her chin on Kaylie's head. She felt the little body grow heavier as sleep finally came. When Kaylie's breathing was deep and regular, Lavender carried her back to bed.

She headed for home when the first brushstrokes of dawn were painting the eastern horizon, preoccupied with her nighttime thoughts, not paying much attention to what was around her. She never noticed the car quietly following her, lights out, to within a couple of blocks of her mother's house.

~*~

Martha was busy, as usual, but somehow the round of non-stop activity wasn't as satisfying as it once was. The failure of her plan to deal with Kevin, her inability to swing that baseball bat, the messy aftermath, haunted her and renewed her sense of humiliation.

Even Lavender was more together than I was. I was just undone. I came apart. Wimped out. And now he's out there somewhere, and he's even more dangerous than before. He knows I'm a coward, and that has to give him power.

Zach noticed something was up. "What's with you these days?" he asked. "You jump like a rabbit every time the phone rings, and you forget things. You never used to do that."

"Must be early menopause," she replied. "Next thing you know I'll be having hot flashes."

"I'm serious, Martha," Zach said. "Even the kids say you're not yourself, and it takes a lot to get those two to notice anything that's not on social media."

Martha fought down an urge to tell him everything. She longed for his sympathy, his rational insight into problems. She'd had a horrible experience, one that seemed to be life-changing, and she wanted to talk it over with her husband. But she didn't dare risk it. Zach had fallen in love with calm, capable Martha. That's who he married. It was hardly fair to change the ground rules at this late date.

So Martha said, "I'm fine, really. Not sleeping too well these days, and I guess it makes me jumpy."

"Why don't you schedule a check-up with Dr. Mills?" Zach said. "You're overdue anyway. Maybe he could give you something to help you sleep."

"Yeah, sure, great idea," Martha said. "I'll call him today."

But she didn't. Kept secrets were safe secrets.

~*~

Did I leave the door between the garage and kitchen unlocked? Lavender wondered, when the doorknob turned without the aid of her key. She felt goose bumps rise on her arms. The locks had been changed after Kevin disappeared; Martha had seen to that. Now there were sturdy deadbolts as well. Only Lavender, Martha and Pat had the new keys. *Must have just forgotten to lock it. Can't panic at every little thing.*

She went in each room, turning on lights, opening closet doors, checking windows and locks. The basement door? No, she couldn't go down there. Surely, there was no need. But just to be on the safe side, she wedged a kitchen chair under the doorknob. She cast an uneasy glance upward at the attic trapdoor as she went down the hall. Being alone in the house was beginning to fray her nerves. Maybe it *was* time to move on. She checked the drawer of her bedside table; yes, the gun was still there.

~*~

Lavender didn't expect the phone call that came at 10 a.m. She was deeply asleep after her night on duty at the Nest. It took her a minute to figure out that the annoying ringing sound meant she had to wake up.

"Yes?" she mumbled.

"Lavender, it's June Gordon. Were you sleeping? I'm sorry if I woke you."

"June, hi. I worked last night. What do you – I mean, what can I do for you?"

"It's a bit of an emergency. I just got a call from WNGN. They're doing a series on domestic violence and want to feature our program on one of their shows. We're beyond excited, as you can imagine. They asked to do an interview with one of our volunteers, and we naturally thought of you first."

"Why me?"

"Because you're doing serious, worthwhile work, and you know how to talk about it. And you're so pretty, Lavender. Didn't you used to be a model? The camera would love you, and the audience would love you."

"When is this interview?"

"Well, actually, it's today. This afternoon. I'm sorry, I know you were up all night, but that makes your story even better. Will you do it?"

"Oh. This afternoon. Well, sure, I want to do whatever it takes to help our clients. Just let me get myself together and tell me when and where."

~*~

Lavender pushed open the plate-glass doors of the local television station promptly at two that afternoon. She'd been assured that a make-up artist would help disguise the dark circles under her eyes, but she'd still done an immaculate make-up job at home. Of course, she was motivated in part by vanity, but mostly she sought the self-confidence that looking good always brought her. What she had to say was important; she wanted to do it justice.

Facing the camera was intimidating at first, but minutes into the interview she forgot it was there. The interviewer, Carol Kline, was a familiar face, having been the anchor of the six o'clock news for years. Despite her Barbie-doll appearance, she was warm and friendly. She knew how to ask open-ended questions that invited a response, beginning with, "How did you get involved with the End Domestic Violence Initiative?"

"I w-was looking for something meaningful to do," Lavender said, mentally cursing the return of her old nervous stammer. "I applied, and they t-trained me, and put me to work nights at the safe house, the Nest. I've met the most wonderful women and k-kids there. They are so brave. These moms have the courage to leave b-bad situations even though their risk often increases when they leave their abusers. That's why the safe house is so important. It gives families a haven to catch their b-breath and figure out what to do next."

"What drew you to this kind of volunteer work?"

"Well, I've had some personal experience with d-domestic violence. I know how scary it is because I was t-terrified when it happened to me. I didn't have children to worry about so it was easy for me to get away – relatively easy – but many of our clients have no money, several kids to uproot from home and school, no family support, and the threat of even greater violence if they leave. The kids just tear my heart out. They're so frightened and confused. Sometimes they've gotten knocked around, too, so they have physical trauma to deal with. I want to take every one of them home with me."

Lavender stopped, out of breath, stammer forgotten.

Carol looked at her sympathetically. "I can see this is very meaningful to you. Tell our audience what they can do to help."

"We always need money," Lavender said. "And volunteers. We need office staffers and fund-raisers, drivers and tutors. Volunteers sort donated clothing and make sure it's clean and mended. We have a little store staffed by volunteers where families can pick up toiletries and clothing, because many families escape with nothing. Almost all the women need jobs, and business people could help them prepare for job interviews. Appropriate clothing is needed so our clients can present themselves professionally. If everyone would get the word out to their civic clubs and community groups, I think employers would come forward and offer to place some of our clients. This community is quick to respond when there is a need, so we need to get our story out there."

~*~

"Lavender, great job!" June said.

They'd gone for coffee after the interview. Now that it was all over, Lavender's nerves kicked in, and the coffee cup jiggled in her hand.

"Carol was so nice," she said, "she made me feel like we were just two friends, talking. I hope I didn't get too carried away."

"Not one bit," June said. "You were passionate and sincere, anyone could see that. This publicity will give us the boost we've needed. With the story running on television, I'm hoping the newspapers will follow-up. If they do, will you be available for print interviews?"

"Sure, whatever you need," Lavender said. She didn't mention that she'd had a disturbing thought. Kevin had been out of sight, but never far from mind. If he saw her interview, would it reignite his wish for revenge?

CHAPTER SIXTEEN

2014

He jingled as he walked, this tall, good-looking policeman. Handcuffs, holster and gun, nightstick, walkie-talkie, and keys were attached to his thick leather belt, turning him into a creaky, leathery wind-chime. His shirt-front was pulled taut over the bullet-proof vest beneath it. Lavender wondered how he could stand to walk around so encumbered all day.

"Are you Lavender McGuire?" he asked.

"I am. And you're Officer Olsen. I was expecting you."

Lavender patted the chair next to hers at the coffee shop table. She'd arranged to meet him as part of the End Domestic Violence Initiative community outreach. Since her television interview, she'd found herself in some demand. Newspaper reporters, television interviewers, one magazine writer, and a woman working on a novel had all asked for her time. The city council invited her to accept a proclamation declaring End Domestic Violence Day. And now this representative of the police department wanted a meeting to talk about ways to keep women safe. As if she knew! As if she wasn't a person who'd been beaten up herself. But somehow, because she was open about it, that experience added to her credibility.

"Please, call me Mike," the policeman said, sitting down and removing his hat. Without it, he looked younger and more approachable. Lavender relaxed. This was just another man, and if there was anything she knew backward and forward, it was how to charm a man. She turned the full force of her lilac gaze upon him.

"I'd like to learn more about what the YWCA program offers," Mike said. "I get calls to domestic violence scenes every shift. We consider it one of our most dangerous situations because emotions are running high and often someone has a weapon. Policy is to try to defuse the situation through talking. If that doesn't work, we generally arrest somebody. Usually it's the man, but not always. I know the YWCA sponsors a safe house, and I'd like to be able to offer it as a suggestion to women who need a place to regroup."

Lavender could talk about the safe house in her sleep and suspected that she sometimes did. She launched into a description of the facility, the intake protocol, services offered and success stories.

"Is it really safe, though?" Mike asked. "Abusers are good at finding their victims."

"I know. We take safety precautions when we transport our clients, but there's always a possibility that someone's abuser will learn where she is. We have staff on duty twenty-four hours a day, the doors are always locked, and the grounds are enclosed by a high privacy fence. We're ready to dial 911 at the first hint of a threat."

"Have you ever had to do that?"

"Yes, twice. The police response was fast and thorough. I felt we were adequately protected."

"The safe house is in my zone, so I might be the responder to the next call. Is there anything I should know about the house or grounds, places where I could be ambushed, for instance?"

"There are no shrubs or outbuildings for that reason. Volunteers park their cars close to the back door, so I suppose someone could crouch down behind a car. Other than that, there's some playground equipment but it's out in the open. There's a remote-controlled access gate. Volunteers call as they get near, and the person on duty opens it. We try to time it so nobody waits in the street for more than a minute, and we all travel with our car doors locked."

"Are volunteers armed?"

Lavender laughed. "No, nobody's packing heat that I know of. It would be a sad commentary on our stated mission, to end violence, if we were ready to shoot someone."

"I don't advocate civilians carrying guns," Mike said, "especially in a situation where there are children. But I wonder if you'd consider having your staff take self-defense classes. The police department offers them quarterly. In the case of the safe house staff, I think the trainers would be willing to add another class especially for them. For you."

Lavender permitted herself an almost imperceptible eyelash flutter. "Why, Mike, that's so kind," she said. "I'll be sure to suggest it at the next staff meeting. Should we get in touch with you, or is there someone else who handles classes?"

"No, I'll be one of the instructors. You can reach me here." He slid his business card across the table, then pulled it back, took out his pen, and wrote a number on the back. "This is my personal cell phone. You can always reach me on it. Don't hesitate to call. I mean it."

Mike cleared his throat, and reassumed his official demeanor. "The police department applauds your efforts to assist victims of domestic violence," he said formally. "Anything we can do to help, we're ready to do it. The main thing is for the volunteers and the clients to remain safe."

He rose, shook Lavender's hand, and, jangling, headed out the door. Lavender watched him go, and then sat staring after him for several moments. She'd have said Mike wasn't her type, but it had been a long time since she'd met a man to whom she felt so instantly attracted.

~*~

"Mike Olsen?" Lavender said.

"Yes, this is Officer Olsen."

"Mike, this is Lavender McGuire. We met –"

"I remember you, Ms. McGuire. Lavender."

"I'm calling about the self-defense classes you offered for our volunteers. The staff is very interested and would like to schedule time."

"That's great. Let me check my calendar at work. I'm off today."

"Oh, I'm sorry to have bothered you on your day off."

"Not a problem. I told you to call any time. It'll be my pleasure to accommodate you, uh, your group. Is there a number where I can reach you?"

Lavender recited her cell phone number, and they exchanged a few more words before hanging up. She looked forward to the classes, not only as an excuse to see the attractive Officer Olsen again, but also as a means of protecting herself. Pat's gun was still in the bedside table at her mother's house, but she had no confidence that she could use it if the need arose. The memory of facing the barrel of the gun in Kevin's hand still made her knees weak.

~*~

"Good evening, ladies, if I may have your attention, please," Mike Olsen said, his voice rising to cut through the chatter of thirty nervous women in the police gymnasium. "I'd like you to divide up into three groups of ten."

There was milling and giggling as the women formed groups. Lavender found herself near the back of the crowd. Mike's eyes scanned the room, and she wondered if he was looking for her. She ducked behind a large woman. Lavender understood the value of anticipation.

"We're here tonight to practice some basic self-defense tactics. I promise, when you've completed this course, you'll feel more confident, and that will automatically make you safer," Mike began. "Attackers look for easy marks that don't seem like they'd put up a fight. One problem that nice folks have is the fear of hurting someone's feelings. Maybe you see a person who gives you a bad vibe, but hey, you might be wrong. You'd feel awful if you insulted an innocent guy and made a scene."

Heads nodded in recognition.

"Well, so what? Your safety is more important than being a polite lady. Your voice is your first weapon. Be ready to yell NO. Be ready to make one hell of a racket. Let me hear you scream."

There were a few half-hearted screams among the laughter of the audience.

"Come on, now, ladies, that won't scare anybody away. Pretend you're protecting a baby. That baby is going to be snatched right out of your arms by an attacker. Now scream!"

Shrieks filled the room and bounced off the walls. Most of the women were mothers; they could get into a scenario like that.

"Much better," Mike said. "If anyone gets into your personal space, look him straight in the eye and yell NO! Remember, he's looking for an easy victim. You don't want to be that person. Let me hear you say NO."

"NO!" the women roared. They didn't look or sound like easy victims.

"Don't hurt *me*, now," Mike said, "I'm one of the good guys."

The women laughed, and Lavender's shoulders relaxed. She'd pushed for the classes and worried they might be a flop that reflected badly on her. But Mike was making this fun *and* informative.

"Many, if not most attackers will back off if you make a scene, so that's your first line of defense," Mike continued. "Better to be embarrassed than mugged."

The class learned about the most vulnerable points on an attacker's body: eyes, groin, knees, nose and neck. They watched Mike demonstrate how to get out of a wrist hold, a head lock, a choke hold. They practiced punching a man wearing a padded suit, yelling at the tops of their lungs while kicking and hitting. The exertion made cheeks rosy and eyes sparkle. The women felt powerful.

Mike brought them back down to earth with a sobering talk about prevention. "Look around you," he said. "Be aware of everyone and everything in your vicinity. Don't get into an elevator if you have a bad feeling about someone who's already on. And don't take the stairs, either. Wait until you can ride with a few more people. Lock your car doors when you're driving and lock your house doors when you're at home. If you meet someone on the street who looks threatening, don't put your head down and avoid eye contact. Look him straight in the eyes. The last thing a mugger wants is a hard time. You want to look like a hard time - a very hard time. Avoid risky situations. You know the drill: ask the mall security guard to walk you to your car at night; head for a police station if you think you're being followed; keep your phone on you at all times and make sure it's charged. The best safety precaution of all is prevention."

After the class ended, Lavender waited at the back of the room until the crowd around Mike finally thinned. There seemed to be a lot questions for the handsome instructor. He answered them all with patient good humor, but he kept glancing up to make sure Lavender was still there.

"So. Do you think the class was helpful?" Mike asked as they walked to the parking deck.

"I think so. Myself, I'd need more practice to feel really confident about the moves you showed us, but at least I have some idea of what to do."

"Just let me know when you have some free time, and I'll be glad to go over it all with you again, one on one. Maybe we could have dinner, too?"

"Well..."

"Or coffee. Just coffee, would that be better?"

"I have no objection to dinner, Mike," Lavender said, smiling. "I like you. It's just that I'm taking time out from dating right now. I made a very bad choice that is still having repercussions in my life, and I'm trying to figure out how I got it so wrong. I don't want to ever make a mistake like that again."

"Fair enough," Mike said. "I'll be around whenever you're ready. In the meantime, I meant what I said about giving you some practice in self-defense. We'll keep it very professional. How's that sound?"

"I'd like that, thank you."

They arranged to meet at the police gym on Mike's next day off. Lavender headed for home, wishing there was someone there to turn on the lights and greet her at the door. Entering the empty house at night gave her the creeps. That was a recent development, and one she didn't like. She'd always been cautious, always played her little game of looking for hiding places wherever she was. But now she was afraid. She hated to admit to herself that Kevin had taken her peace of mind with him when he disappeared.

CHAPTER SEVENTEEN

2014

Martha woke in a sweaty tangle of sheets. A look at the clock showed nine a.m. She couldn't remember when she'd last slept so late. Zach and the kids must have gotten themselves off without her help. She wondered idly if anyone had had breakfast.

Cha-cha peered at Martha over the edge of the bed. Named for her habit of doing an intricate dance while finding the perfect spot to urinate, she was a pound puppy with the most persuasive eyes in the universe. Martha could feel thought beams directed from Cha-cha's mind to hers: *get up, feed me, get up, feed me.*

Okay, okay, Martha thought back, moving herself by inches into a sitting position. When did she get so stiff and sore from just sleeping? It hadn't been a restful night. She remembered looking at the clock at 1:39, 3:14 and 6:11. The curse of digital clocks was that you not only knew what time it was to the minute, the orange numbers were permanently down-loaded into your brain.

Maybe she was getting sick. Her stomach felt a little iffy and her feet protested being put onto the floor by shooting pains right up her ankles. She fell back into bed, only to be confronted again by Cha-cha's accusing brown gaze.

Finally, she made it to the kitchen, let the dog out into the back yard for her morning dance, dumped some dry food in her dish, and poured herself the first cup of coffee. Another day was officially underway. Martha dreaded it.

She, of the lists and agendas, had gradually run down like a clock someone forgot to wind. Now she found herself with nothing she wanted to do. The house certainly needed a good going-over, and weeds were fast erasing her flower beds. But who cared? Grocery shopping must be done, some kind of dinner must be put on the table tonight. But who cared? A look at the old-school paper calendar pinned to the refrigerator with magnets showed that she had a dentist appointment that afternoon. She picked up the phone and cancelled it. No, she wouldn't like to reschedule at this time. Who cared?

Martha knew she was stuck, but she felt powerless to do anything about it. Zach kept saying she just needed a good rest and it was no wonder, doing all she normally did. He was being supportive and patient in an off-hand way, but sooner or later he'd expect her to pull herself together. The kids hardly noticed her and probably hadn't missed her presence in their daily lives. Cha-cha was the only creature who depended on Martha totally. Even Lavender had moved on, volunteering at the safe house, and going on television and everything. Tears of self-pity filled Martha's eyes. No one appreciated her. No one cared if she lived or died. God, she was sick of herself.

Maybe she should make an appointment for a check-up, as Zach suggested. But the thought of baring her soul to their family doctor, whom she regularly saw at parties, was too embarrassing. She needed someone who didn't know her at all. Booting up her computer, she typed "psychiatrists" in the search engine. A list of names appeared. She picked the first female name she saw and dialed the number without giving herself time to think about it.

Probably can't get in for months, she thought. But the receptionist said, "Dr. Bachmann just had a cancellation. I don't suppose you could come in at eleven today?"

"Today? No. Yes, I guess I could."

She'd have to shower, wash her hair and find something to wear. Put Cha-cha in the basement, take a package of hamburger out of the freezer to thaw for dinner – sloppy Joes, maybe. Make sure there was gas in her car. She only had an hour. Martha felt a familiar stirring of energy. She had a purpose at last.

~*~

Dr. Bachmann had soulful brown eyes that reminded Martha of Cha-cha's. She shook Martha's hand briskly and gestured to a pair of armchairs in a sunny corner of the room.

"No couch?" Martha said, hoping a joke would ease her nervousness.

"No couch," Dr. Bachmann said with a smile. "Just two people getting to know each other. I'll go first. I'm Leah Bachmann. My medical degree is from Harvard, and I've been practicing psychiatry for seven years. My husband and I recently had our first child, a little girl. I'm learning to balance home and work, and have a new understanding of how difficult it can be. Now it's your turn."

Martha was disarmed by this doctor's unusual willingness to drop the professional shield of anonymity. "I'm Martha Rendell," she said. "I'm married with two teenage boys, and I've lived in the same house for twenty years."

"What brings you to see me, Martha?"

"Are we done getting to know each other already?" Martha asked.

"We're just beginning. But our time together is precious, and, for you, expensive, so I like to get right to the point whenever possible. Maybe you're not quite sure why you're here, but give me your best guess."

"I'm undergoing some life experiences with which I need help," Martha said, and sat back waiting for approval. She'd practiced this line in the car driving over.

Dr. Bachmann looked at her.

"See, some things have happened lately, and I don't feel like myself anymore," Martha felt compelled to add.

There was silence. Martha couldn't stand it.

"I'm not who I thought I was," she blurted, and to her horror felt her throat tighten, and her eyes brim with hot tears.

"Oh, no," she said, "I'm such an ugly crier. Sorry, sorry."

Dr. Bachmann silently offered a box of tissues. Martha took one and mopped her face. She managed a shaky smile to show she was fine, just fine. Dr. Bachmann regarded her tranquilly.

"Tell me who you thought you were," she said.

"Well, I'm...I was the strong one. I have a younger sister, Lavender, who's always been such a mess. She's beautiful, and she gets by on her looks, never developed any backbone, never took charge of her life, no career, just lives off the current boyfriend. I've always had to look out for Lavender; our mother drilled that into me from the start. And sometimes it wasn't much fun, but I always did it."

"I see. And what's changed that makes you feel you are different now?"

"Well, you wouldn't believe...It's a long story...It's crazy, actually."

"Tell me."

Martha gathered her thoughts, sat up straight, and began. "Lavender had this boyfriend, Kevin. She was living with him, having quite the high life with nights on the town and new clothes and trips. But he beat her, and she took some money from him and ran away. Then our mother died and Lavender had to come home. Kevin started stalking her. I was so mad! How dare he hurt my sister? I made a plan." She stopped.

"Yes. What was your plan?"

"It sounds so stupid. I hate to say it."

Dr. Bachmann waited.

"Lavender was – is – living in Mom's house. I took her to stay with Aunt Pat, and then I dressed up like her, like Lavender, and hid in the attic. I planned to, well, to lure Kevin up there, and beat him with a baseball bat."

Martha stole a glance at Dr. Bachmann. She was gazing out the window. Her face looked interested but not shocked.

"I know; it's so stupid, right? I can't even believe I planned it, and almost did it. God, what was I thinking? I'm not the kind of person who gets in fights."

"We are all fighters when it comes to defending what we love," Dr. Bachmann said.

"But then I choked," Martha continued. "Kevin would have beaten me with my own baseball bat except he slipped on the stairs – well, I kind of shoved him – and he fell and got hurt pretty bad. And what did I do? I called Aunt Pat and

Lavender – Lavender! – to rescue *me*." Martha's face burned with shame at the memory.

"And did they rescue you?"

"They took over. Lavender was so calm, and it was she who decided what we had to do next. I followed along. I couldn't think; I was helpless. Ever since then, I haven't felt like myself. At first, it was a relief to think I didn't always have to be in charge. But if I'm not that person, then I don't know who I am."

"Would your mother be angry with you if she knew what happened?" Dr. Bachmann asked.

Martha blinked. "Yes, I think she would be. I failed Lavender. That was never supposed to happen."

"But then Lavender stepped up, didn't she? You said she took over, and it sounded like that never happened before."

"I guess it didn't. Either Mom or I always jumped in and fixed whatever was wrong for Lavender."

"So maybe your Mom would have been surprised at first, but then happy that Lavender handled a difficult situation?"

"Yes, but *I* couldn't handle it. *I* failed."

"Talk more about how that makes you feel."

"I feel...I feel like an incompetent idiot, like a total failure. Whoever this new me is, I don't like her."

CHAPTER EIGHTEEN

2014

"Hit me hard! Put your body weight into it," Mike yelled through his face mask. Lavender punched his padded arm as hard as she could. Pain shot from her hand to her shoulder.

"What good did that do?" Mike asked. "Did it immobilize me? Nope, I'm still coming at you. You've got to go for the body parts where I'm vulnerable: eyes, throat, crotch, knees. Now come on. Try it again."

Lavender was sweating. Her hair clung damply to her head and her tee shirt was soaked. Was this self-defense lesson never going to end? When she'd told Mike she needed more practice to feel confident about defending herself, she hadn't had this in mind. Maybe a few jabs, a few laughs, and a break for coffee. But he was relentless.

"Come on, wussy girl," he taunted. "Show me what you got, if you got anything. A baby could hit harder than you." He reached out with his big glove and tapped her face none too gently.

"Dammit!" Lavender said, angry tears stinging her eyes. "You're b-bigger than I am, you bully."

"Oh, I see, then we'll only allow small muggers to attack you," Mike replied, tapping her chin a little harder.

Enraged, Lavender flew at him, aiming her fist at his throat, followed by stiff fingers in his eyes.

"That's more like it," he said, "That's my girl. Oof!"

The oof was when she doubled him up – padded suit and all – with a well-aimed kick in the groin. He straightened and grabbed her from behind in a bear hug. She countered as he'd taught her, by squatting and leaning back into him. Her weight threw him off balance; she twisted out of his grip and ran.

"That's great," Mike gasped, "you don't want to slug it out with me, you want to get away. Whew! Well done." He stripped off his face mask and pulled a glove off with his teeth.

Lavender glared at him. She was still mad enough to punch him. "Boy, you think you know someone!" she said. "Then you find out he's really a big jerk."

"All in the training," Mike said, laughing at her. "You had to get mad to find your fighting spirit. But once you found it, you beat the crap out of me. Without this padded suit, I'd be on the floor."

"Really? Well, good. That's where you belong." Lavender swept by him on her way to the women's locker room. Standing under a hot shower, she let the spray beat on her lower back, which she'd strained with that ferocious kick. She towel-dried her hair, didn't bother with make-up, dressed in clean sweats and headed out the door. Mike was waiting for her.

"How about that coffee now?" he asked.

"No, thanks," she replied. "I've got to go."

"You're not mad, are you? I'm just trying to teach you how to defend yourself. That's what you said you wanted."

"Yeah, well, great job."

She felt his eyes on her as she marched out the door, wishing the pneumatic closing mechanism would allow her to slam it. Once in her car, she calmed down. It wasn't fair to be mad at Mike, she admitted to herself. He was only doing what she'd asked: teaching her self-defense. Still, what an annoying person he'd turned out to be.

Hunger twisted her belly, and she suddenly wanted food. She aimed her car at the nearest drive-through, pulled up to the curbside microphone, and ordered a cheeseburger. "And fries," she added, "and a milkshake." The response was a garbled warbling sound. She repeated her order and got the same warbling.

"Well, darn," she said aloud, pulling her car into a parking space. So much for the drive-through; she'd have to go inside. Walking to the entrance, she met a crowd of teenage boys, jostling and punching each other. When they saw her, they burst into wolf whistles and cat-calls.

"Hey, mama! Let me give you a happy meal," one of them called, to the delight of his friends.

Lavender was in no mood for it. She stopped in her tracks, and turned to face the group. Adrenalin still pumped through her veins. She looked the leader straight in the eyes, and then stared at each boy in turn. Not a word was spoken. Laughter dried up. Nervous shuffling replaced the high-five-slapping bonhomie of a minute ago. Lavender held their gaze for another few seconds, then turned, and went through the door.

By golly, it worked! She couldn't wait to tell someone.

~*~

"And then I just stared them down," Lavender recounted to Martha. "It was like Mike said, they backed off."

"But was that a safe thing to do?" Martha asked. "What if they hadn't backed off? You couldn't take on all of them at once. You don't want to get too cocky."

"You're right, I know you're right. But it felt so good to be strong and not afraid. Did you ever stop and think how often you feel scared when you're out by yourself? How many times do you hit the door locks in your car when you come to a stoplight and there are people on the corner? How often do you duck into a store or cross the street to avoid somebody who looks iffy?"

"Well, sure, but that's just common sense. You shouldn't pick a fight."

"No, but it's a really great feeling to think if a fight *is* picked, I can handle it."

Martha looked down at her hands clasped passively in her lap. "I guess," she said in a small voice.

"What's wrong, Sis? You've been different lately. Ever since Kevin, really."

"Yeah. I don't know. I don't feel like myself. Doesn't it bother you, all that happened with him?"

"I think about it some. But good came of it. I haven't seen him around since, so that's positive. And the whole thing led me to my volunteer job at the safe house, and turned my life in a new direction."

"I know. I'm glad for you."

"But?"

"But what if he comes back? We don't know where he

is or what he's up to."

"If he comes back, I'll handle it," Lavender said.

"Who *are* you?" Martha asked, "and what have you done with my little Pee-Pot Lav?"

"Pee-Pot's still here, Sis. Maybe she's just growing up. Finally."

~*~

Despite the flurry of publicity with which she'd been involved for the End Domestic Violence Initiative, Lavender was unprepared for the phone call she received the next day from June Gordon.

"Can you come in to the office before you start your shift at the Nest?" June asked.

"Sure, I guess," Lavender replied. "What's up?"

"Let's wait until you get here," June said.

Mystified, Lavender presented herself in June's office at the appointed time.

"I hope I haven't done something wrong," she began.

"No, no, not at all," June said. "In fact, you've done a lot of things right. Board members have been calling me because they've seen your interview on television, or read a print article about you."

"I'm sorry, has it been too much?" Lavender asked. "I thought it would be good to get our story out there at every opportunity. I didn't mean to be a publicity hog."

"Lavender, let me finish. The board met yesterday and discussed something that's been in the works for a while. The Nest needs a permanent resident house mother. Someone who'd make the house her home and supervise its operations day-to-day. The volunteers we have are absolutely great and we'd still need them. But what we've been lacking is continuity, and that could come from having one person in charge. They want that person to be you."

"Me? Wow. Live there full-time? That sounds like I'd always be working."

"That's why we'd continue to have volunteers staff the intake desk," June said. "What you'd do is oversee the nuts and bolts of running of the place: ordering groceries and supplies, keeping track of paperwork, coordinating the volunteers. And of course, interacting with the residents. We already know how good you are with them."

"Would I have a room in the house, like everyone else?"

"There's actually great attic space. The Board is willing to fund the creation of a bedroom and bath in the attic for the housemother. You'd be on the scene but not always in it, if you know what I mean. There's a salary. It's not very much, but you'd have no living expenses."

"But don't you need someone with a degree in social work or something?"

"That would be ideal. There is tuition reimbursement for you to study for that degree if you choose."

"It sounds interesting. I'm flattered that you thought of me. Could I have twenty-four hours to think about it?"

"Of course. We expect you to sleep on it before you decide. We hope you'll take the job, but if you don't, we don't want to lose you as a volunteer. Get back to me tomorrow, okay?"

~*~

Ordinarily, Lavender would have gone straight to Martha to talk over this new wrinkle in her life. But Martha was acting so strangely these days that Lavender hesitated.

Instead, she called Pat.

Sitting in Pat's crowded kitchen with just enough space cleared on the table for their teacups and Girl Scout cookies, she related her conversation with June Gordon.

"So, you see, I'd be there every day and night. I'd have a private living space, but I'd always be on call if there was an emergency. Everyone would get to depend on me more and more. Sounds like it would be hard to have a private life, go on dates or whatever. It wouldn't be glamorous, that's for sure."

"So what's the downside?" Pat said, with a broad grin.

"That *is* the downside."

"Let's think about this. You'd have a salary – any health benefits?"

"I don't know, June didn't say."

"Okay, that's something you want to ask. Let's suppose you do have some kind of group insurance, which is more than you've ever had in your adult life. So you get a paycheck, and you can go to the doctor if you're sick. You have a place to live, and work that you already know you love. I doubt you'd be expected to be in the house twenty-four hours a day. That's something else you want to clarify: exactly what kind of hours would you be expected to put in. But I think all this would become clear as you did it. You'd be creating the job; no one else has had it before you. So you'd make it your own."

"I do love the work as a volunteer, but would I still love it if I was in charge?"

"What do you love about it?"

"Well, the people, of course. The moms are scared, and yet strong. And the little kids just bop right into my heart. You and I have never been mothers, Aunt Pat, and I never thought

I wanted children. But now I have to rethink that because of these kids."

Pat nodded. "I've never regretted my choice to remain single and childless, but you and Martha are natural-born mothers."

"Me?" Lavender asked, startled. "I mean, Martha, yes, she's a great mom, but I've just been, I don't know, drifting."

"You are an accepting, tolerant person. You're kind and helpful without being bossy and intrusive. Those would be great qualities in a mother. I think you've turned a corner in your personal life since Kevin."

The mention of his name made both women quiet for a minute.

"Look at the way you took charge of that debacle," Pat continued. "Martha was freaked out, and I didn't know what to do, either, but you stepped up."

"Yeah, and eventually got a gun pointed at my head for my troubles."

"True. There are few redeeming qualities for Kevin."

"That's one reason I don't trust my ability to make decisions," Lavender said. "Look at the decision I made to be with him."

"But you learned from it," Pat said. "That's really all we can ask of ourselves, that we learn from our mistakes. I'd say congratulate yourself on knowing when to hold 'em and when to fold 'em. It's never good to make decisions out of fear, so this shouldn't be the main factor, but something to consider: you'd be safe from Kevin if you lived in the Nest."

"So you think he's still a threat?"

"Who knows? But I'd sleep better at night if I knew you were someplace safe."

~*~

Lavender thought of one other person whose feedback would be useful as she made her decision: Mike. Her irritation with him forgotten, she rifled through her purse until she found the dog-eared card he'd given her. She called his personal cell phone number, scrawled on the back of the card.

"Officer Mike Olsen," he answered, sounding so official that she hesitated.

"Uh, Mike, it's Lavender. Am I catching you at a busy time?"

"Oh, hi, Lavender. Good to hear from you. I'm at work right now. What's up?"

"I'd like to talk with you about something. If you have time."

"I'll always have time for you. I get off at four. Where shall we meet?"

"Could you come to my mother's house? That's where I live right now. We could talk without interruption there."

She gave him the address, and at four fifteen his car pulled into the drive. He emerged in jeans and a flannel shirt, looking much more approachable without the full panoply of law enforcement equipment. Like a regular guy, she thought. She led him into the living room, where he stopped short at the sight of the alphabet quilt draped over the back of the sofa.

"Where'd you get that?" he asked.

"We found the blocks in an old trunk, and my Aunt Pat and I finished it. Why? Do you like quilts?"

"My mother is a quilt fanatic. Her house is full of them, hanging on walls, over beds, covering chairs, everywhere. I think I've seen one similar to this one in a crib she keeps for possible grandchildren."

"Possible grandchildren? Don't you have brothers and sisters to help out on that front?"

"Nope, I'm an only. No pressure or anything, but Mom has one of her spare bedrooms fixed up as a nursery just in case I ever get around to giving her grands."

"Right, no pressure there," Lavender said. They laughed.

"What did you want to talk to me about?" Mike asked.

Lavender told him about the job opportunity at the safe house, reciting all the pros and cons she could think of.

"I don't know whether to take it or not," she finished.

"Why wouldn't you take it?" Mike asked. "Sounds great to me."

"Well, but it would be a very responsible position. Maybe not much time off. Sounds like I'd need to get at least a bachelor's degree if I continue with it. And I might get tired of living where I work."

"No way of knowing that until you've done it. As for being responsible, you're a big girl. You can handle whatever comes your way." Mike spoke matter-of-factly. She realized he wasn't trying to flatter her.

"You think? You think I can handle anything?" she asked.

"Of course. You beat the snot out of me in your second self-defense class."

"I was mad!" Lavender said. "But real life is different. I've never been good at handling things."

"You seem good at handling things to me," Mike said. "I'd say go for this job. It sounds perfect for you. If it isn't, then you make a new plan."

"Sounds simple, the way you put it."

"It is simple. Don't over think it, just do it."

And so Lavender did.

CHAPTER NINETEEN

2014

Martha continued to see Dr. Bachmann regularly. Wednesdays at eleven became her time slot, and she found herself looking forward to her sessions. Dr. Bachmann didn't fit the mold that Martha's mind had constructed of a typical psychiatrist. She was younger, prettier, and not at all averse to stating her opinion. Martha'd had a mental picture of an elderly man with a slight foreign accent, whose only comment was, "Hmmmm." Dr. Bachmann ("Call me Leah") started some of her sentences with, "Would you consider..." To which Martha would often answer, "Yes, but..." and Leah would smile and change the subject.

On this day, Martha was talking again about Lavender's charmed life. "She's never had an actual job, well, except for the modeling. But that was more like play for her. She made good money, but she didn't try to get more jobs, didn't even take all the jobs the agency sent her way. And when a man beckoned, she chucked it all and went with him."

"Why do you think Lavender's behavior back then still

bothers you today?" Leah asked.

"Why? Well, obviously, it was irresponsible, and then I had to pick up the pieces."

"Tell me about those pieces."

"I had to quit my job, break our lease in New York, make arrangements to move all our stuff back home, get back my old teaching job here, find a new apartment, and get settled again," Martha said in an angry sing-song.

"That was a lot. I think you mentioned you also met your husband in New York."

"Yes, that's where I met Zach, at the school where we both taught. That was one good thing that came of it."

"And you loved your teaching job there?"

"I did. The school was in the inner city, full of kids I never would have met if I'd stayed home. I wouldn't take anything for that experience...." Martha's voice trailed away. "So why don't I focus on the good things instead of always just the bad?"

There was silence. Silence used to throw Martha and make her babble to fill it, but she'd learned it was valuable thinking time. She fought the urge to fidget and made herself as still as possible.

"You know, I'm just realizing that I've talked more about Lavender than about myself the whole time I've been coming here."

Leah nodded thoughtfully. As usual, her face was composed and interested. She never seemed bored or hurried or judgmental. She said, "Are you still angry at Lavender?"

"No, of course not. She's my sister. I love her."

"Yes. But are you angry with her?"

Silence. Martha got up and paced the length of the office and back several times. Finally: "Yes. Yes! She makes me so damn mad. She's like a big baby, always expecting me to fix things."

"Do you think she expects that of you today?"

"Maybe not so much lately. Like I've said, she seems to have gotten herself together. She even told me she's finally grown up. I wish I could count on that. Now she's all over television and magazines for her volunteer work with battered women, but just wait, sooner or later she'll revert to her old pattern and I'll be drawn right back into her chaos."

"So now is not so bad; it was in the past that you were overburdened with Lavender's problems."

"Yeah, I guess so," Martha said slowly.

"Your mother insisted on it, yes? Are you angry with her?"

"With my mother? She's dead. You can't be angry with a dead person."

"Can't you?"

Profound silence. Martha felt a flush rise up her neck and color her face a hot red. Sweat broke out along her hairline. Her breath caught in her chest. Again, she got up from her chair abruptly and walked around the office.

"Why don't you tell me what you're feeling right now?" Leah said.

"I can't."

Silence. Martha was crying in great gulping sobs. She no longer apologized for being an ugly crier. Too many tears had been shed in this room for that to matter. Leah waited.

"My damn mother!" Martha shouted. "I don't think she

even cared about me, it was all Lavender, Lavender, Lavender, day and night. I was expected to drop whatever I was doing and rescue Lavender and never complain or say a bad word about her. Dad knew it wasn't fair, he talked to me about it a couple of times, but he'd just say, 'Do it for your Mom, Martha.' He didn't care about me, either, only about keeping Mom happy."

Martha sank back down in her chair facing Leah. Shaken and exhausted by her outburst, she just wanted to go home. She reached for her purse, but Leah put up a hand.

"Let's talk more about this, Martha."

"My hour is up."

Leah walked to her desk, picked up the phone, and spoke quietly to her secretary. She returned to her chair. "Now. We have time."

"I'm too tired."

"Push through it. How do you feel right this minute?"

"Exhausted. Sad. Sorry I said those things about my family."

"You get to be exhausted and sad. But you don't get to be sorry for voicing your feelings. Feelings need to come out, just as a splinter festering in your finger would need to come out."

Martha laid her head back, closed her eyes and willed herself to be calm, but the tears seeped under her eyelashes anyway. "What I wanted never mattered. *I* never mattered, except as Lavender's caretaker. All the striving I did, the good grades, and clubs and sports, it was all to show Mom and Dad that I was the good child, the successful one. But it was never enough; they still loved Lavender more."

"I doubt that," Leah said. "They worried more about

her, certainly, and that can look like love. But you were the rock of the family, the one they could count on. You were more like a parent than a sister to Lavender. And because you were so good at it – at everything – they all took you for granted. Failed to consider your needs or appreciate what you sacrificed, what it cost you. That hurt."

Martha felt an unknotting deep inside. At last, her pain, her struggles were acknowledged, put into words, validated.

"It did hurt," she said. "It still does. I had to make myself a hard shell so I could bear it. I prided myself on being tough-minded, able to handle anything. But now...something's changed. I feel like I'm cracking apart."

"Yes. And where the cracks are, that's where the light shines in."

~*~

Martha made a date with her husband. He looked surprised. Astonished, really. It had been years since they'd made the effort to get out of the house just to be alone together.

"What do you want to do?" he asked.

"Nothing special. Just get some dinner in a place where we won't be rushed. Maybe take a walk in the park afterwards."

"Do you want to see a movie?" Zach seemed unable to remember what their nights out used to be like.

"No, I'd like to just talk."

"Just talk. Okay."

They went to a French restaurant, one that specialized in unhurried dining. A meal there took hours because everything was fresh and cooked only when ordered. Martha wanted those long intervals between courses. She had some things to say.

"I guess you've noticed that I haven't been myself lately," she began.

"Yeah, you have been kind of off. Are you feeling better?" Zach said.

"Better about some things, worse about others. I need to tell you something. There was this thing that happened. Remember when I went on the basket-weaving weekend?"

"Yeah."

"Well, that wasn't where I was."

"What? Where were you, then?"

"I was at Mom's house. Lavender needed –"

"Stop right there," Zach said. "How much does she need this time? I don't want to know what happened, and I don't want to spend the whole evening talking about Lavender. Just tell me how much to write the check for."

"No, she doesn't need money this time. And it's not about Lavender – well, it started that way, but, really, it's about me. It's hard for me to say this, so let me finish."

Their food sat untouched before them as Martha told Zach about Lavender's abuse at Kevin's hands, Martha's plan for revenge, her inability to follow through, Kevin's injuries, recuperation, and disappearance, and Aunt Pat's involvement. Zach's face was incredulous, but he let her talk without interruption.

"I know, it sounds crazy as bedbugs. I think I *was* a little crazy – maybe I still am. So I've been seeing a psychiatrist," Martha said, "and she's helped me realize some things about myself, things I need to change. I'm asking for your help."

There was a long pause. Zach's gaze was fixed on the far wall. Finally he spoke.

"So let me get this straight. You went on a secret, murderous rampage, injured a man, nursed him back to health, and then started seeing a shrink, all without a word to me, your husband. Why didn't you talk to me?"

She could see a vein throbbing in his forehead, never a good sign.

"Why lie to me and make up such an elaborate cover story?" he continued. "And that was the dumbest, most dangerous, ridiculous plan in the history of the world! What the hell were you thinking? If you'd come to me, I could have helped you see how crazy it was. I could have stopped you."

"You've had to pick up the slack so often for Lavender, I thought this time I wouldn't bother you with her problems," Martha said.

"It was your problem, too."

"I made it my problem," Martha agreed. "But Dr. Bachmann is helping me learn to draw a line between Lavender and me. I've got all I can handle just living my own life."

"I'm furious that you deceived me," Zach said through gritted teeth.

Martha shrank back in her chair. He was so seldom angry with her. In fact, when she stopped to think about it, he'd not had any kind of emotional reaction to her lately. At least he was engaged now. This was no time to cower. She made herself sit up, and meet his eyes.

"I don't blame you for being mad. I'm sorry. You mean more to me than anyone on earth. Please forgive me."

Zach looked away. He cracked his knuckles, a tension-reliever that drove her crazy. There was silence between them, but Martha knew about silences now. She let it be. Finally he turned back to her.

"I can't say I forgive you and mean it right now. I don't know when I'll be able to trust you again. I've got a lot to think about."

"I get that. I understand I have to earn your trust back. You have every right to be mad, but please, Zach, help me. I'm scared I won't be able to handle the changes I need to make. Or that I'll become a different person than the one you married. Maybe you won't love the new me. The worst thing would be to lose our way as a couple."

"In all our years together, I've never heard you admit to being scared of anything," Zach said. "You've always been so tough, so together that it's actually been intimidating. For a while now, I've felt you didn't need me, that I was just an old habit you couldn't be bothered to break."

"Oh, Zach. Not true, so not true."

She reached across the table, and after a long moment he took her hand. The waiter approached, eyeing the untouched plates disapprovingly.

"All finished?" he asked. "Shall I remove these dishes?"

"No," Martha said, "we've just begun."

CHAPTER TWENTY

2015

Lavender woke in her room under the eaves, looking around with sleep-confused eyes at the exposed beams, carpeted floor and *en suite* bathroom visible through an open door. The alphabet quilt hung from a dowel rod set in the space between dormer windows. She'd just spent the first night in her new room at the safe house, and now she was about to embark on her debut as director. She pulled the duvet over her head, and squinched her eyes shut. *Too hard. Can't do it.* But then she remembered she'd promised Kaylie she'd eat breakfast with her. She unwound herself from the sheets and headed for the bathroom.

The aroma of pancakes greeted her when she made her way down the attic stairs and into the common kitchen. One mother stood at the stove. Two more sat at the table, urging their children to hurry up and eat because it was almost time to go to school. Lavender accepted a cup of coffee and sat down at the table, returning smiles and good mornings. Kaylie bounded into the room, her hair done up in pigtails tied with pink bows. She made a bee-line for Lavender and clambered onto the chair beside her.

"Miss Lavender, Miss Lavender, do you see my piggies?" she said. "Mama made me piggies with pink bows."

"I see them. So pretty. And you're all dressed up in that nice dress. Are you and Mama going someplace today?"

"We're going to court," Kaylie said, her eyes big with the gravity of it.

Kaylie's mother, Rhonda, appeared, smoothing her hair, and tugging at her unaccustomed skirt. Like most of the women in the house, her daily uniform was jeans or sweats and sneakers. Wearing a skirt and good shoes meant serious business was at hand.

"Are you all set?" Lavender asked her. "Do you want to leave Kaylie here with me?"

"My lawyer said to bring her. It's hard for a judge not to feel sympathy for kids. We'll catch the bus," Rhonda said.

"Is that safe?"

"Well..."

"Look, why don't I drive you? I'll drop you off at the court house, and you can call my cell when you're ready to come back here."

"I guess it would be better if we stayed off public transportation today," Rhonda said. "My ex may be looking for us. This is a day he said would never come."

"But here it is," Lavender said, "and you deserve all the credit. You've been incredibly brave, and now you're about to become legally free of a bad situation."

"Legal freedom doesn't always translate to freedom in the real world," Rhonda said.

"What's the weal world?" Kaylie asked.

"It's right here and now," Lavender said, "and you and

your Mama are safe. And now you're going to eat pancakes!"

~*~

She dropped Rhonda and Kaylie off at the foot of the courthouse steps, waved goodbye, and promised to keep her cell phone close so she wouldn't miss hearing it ring when they called her to return. Pausing for a moment before pulling back into traffic, she enjoyed the sight of Kaylie taking the steps in two-footed jumps, her pigtails bobbing above her narrow little shoulders. Rhonda's head turned from side to side as she scanned the area. Lavender knew she was looking for her soon-to-be ex-husband, who had threatened that she'd never live to divorce him.

Just as she turned on her signal and edged forward, she caught a flash of movement out of the corner of her eye and heard a loud pop. Instinctively, she hit the brake and threw the car into park. People were yelling and running toward the center of the steps. There was a tiny bundle of pink, curled into the protective circle of a mother's arms. Lavender left her car door swinging wide into traffic and raced up the steps. She saw the widening puddle of dark blood before she reached them.

Her vision narrowed so that all she saw was mother and child. Kaylie held up her arms to be picked up, but Rhonda was very still. "Here," she said to one of the women standing by with her hands over her mouth, eyes wide in horror. "Take her." She thrust Kaylie at her.

Ripping off her belt, she found the source of the bleeding in Rhonda's thigh. *Femoral artery*. Later, she'd ask herself how she knew that. Bright blood pumped in spurts, making the steps slippery. Lavender knelt and fastened her belt around Rhonda's leg above the bullet hole, pulling it as tight as she could. The bleeding slowed to a trickle. Rhonda was shaking. Someone handed her a jacket, and Lavender wrapped it around the wounded woman, but the shivering continued.

"Rhonda!" Lavender said loudly. "Listen to me. You've been shot, but you're going to live. Kaylie is okay, she's not hurt. The ambulance is coming. Do you hear the sirens? Stay with me, Rhonda. Kaylie needs you."

Rhonda's hands gripped Lavender's, her eyes blind with panic. Lavender kept talking until the paramedics arrived. She stepped back to make way for them, but stayed in Rhonda's field of vision.

"I have Kaylie," she said, reaching for her. "See, she's right here in my arms. I'll take care of her."

The panic left Rhonda's eyes. She nodded slightly. The paramedics stabilized her head, then slid her expertly onto a backboard and moved down the steps to the waiting ambulance.

Lavender became aware that Kaylie was whimpering quietly. She'd have felt better if the little girl had been roaring at the top of her voice.

"Red," Kaylie said.

Lavender realized that her hands, arms, and clothing were covered in Rhonda's blood. Her stomach flipped. She sat down suddenly, clutching Kaylie tightly. The little girl began to sob, which Lavender took as a good sign that shock was giving way to fear and sorrow. "I've got you," she crooned, "You're safe with me." There were just the two of them in the world.

Gradually, Lavender became aware of the commotion surrounding her. A man, presumably the shooter, presumably Rhonda's husband, was being hustled into a squad car, hands cuffed behind his back. She tried to stand, but her feet slipped in the slick pool of blood. An arm went around her waist, lifting her and Kaylie effortlessly.

"I've got you," Mike said in her ear. "You're safe with me."

~*~

It was evening and Lavender was back at the Nest. She'd spent the day at the hospital, waiting to hear that Rhonda's surgery had gone well, and that she was, in hospital parlance, resting comfortably. The nurses provided a set of scrubs so she could change out of her blood-soaked clothes. She'd kept Kaylie with her, entertaining her with trips to the cafeteria and vending machines. The hospital chaplain brought a coloring book and blew up rubber gloves for balloons, but inevitably the little girl had grown tired, bored and cranky. It had been a long, bewildering day. When they finally got back to the Nest, Kaylie didn't protest when Lavender tucked her in bed in a room with another mother and child. If she woke during the night, she wouldn't be alone.

Now Lavender sat with June in the kitchen, sipping tea liberally laced with whiskey. Although alcohol was strictly forbidden in the house, June produced a little airline bottle from her purse. She said if she ever saw someone who needed a drink, it was Lavender. The women sat in weary silence for a few minutes.

"Quite a first day," June said.

"What did I do wrong?" Lavender asked. "How could I have prevented what happened to Rhonda?"

"Excuse me, I didn't realize I was having tea with God," June said.

"Well, no, but I should have protected them."

"I wish we *could* protect them away from here. We

can't, it's just that simple. You drove them to the courthouse steps. There's a strong police presence at the courthouse. Rhonda got shot anyway. If the police can't stop this kind of violence, we're wrong to think that somehow we should. That's why there's a safe house, Lavender."

"But poor little Kaylie."

"Kaylie will have her mother back soon. Their lives are safe now that dear old Dad is in the slammer. They can move out of here and start over."

"They'll move out. Of course. I wasn't thinking very far ahead. I'll miss that little girl."

"A word of warning, Lavender. Don't get too attached to your clients. A certain professional detachment is necessary to keep you from burning to a crisp the first year. It's like raising children: your goal is to help them be strong and self-sufficient so they can leave you."

Lavender nodded, suddenly yawning hugely. "Oh, sorry," she said. "I guess my day is catching up with me."

"Time for bed," June said. "I'm tired, too, and my excitement was only vicarious. We'll sort through all of this tomorrow. For now, off you go."

Lavender climbed the steep stairs to her attic hideaway with leaden feet. The room felt shadowy and foreign. She longed for home. But where was that? Her mother's house? That wasn't really home anymore. In her mind's eye, she saw the succession of hotel rooms and apartments in which she'd lived with the various men in her life. For the first time, she longed for her own place, a sanctuary, a personal nest. She imagined a cottage, quilts, a shaggy dog, and good smells from the kitchen. Maybe a child, a little girl like Kaylie, bent over homework at the table. A good man watching football on television, cutting the grass, helping the child learn to ride a bike. Maybe Mike?

~*~

Martha was doing a crossword puzzle while watching the eleven o'clock news with half an eye. That way, she explained to Zach, she could waste her time doing two things badly at once.

"You're just a multi-tasking maniac," he said with a smile.

He seemed a little less strained each day. They spent more time together than they had in years, going for evening walks instead of submersing themselves in television or hobbies. On those walks, they talked with an open heartedness she realized hadn't existed in their marriage for a long time. They'd continued to share a bed, but Zach turned his back and slept as far away from her as he could. Last night he'd reached for her for the first time since her confession. She hoped it signaled a return to normal, or at least to a new normal, in their relationship.

The phone at Martha's elbow vibrated. Glancing at the Caller ID screen, she saw it was Pat. She picked it up and said, "Hi, Aunt Pat. It's late; is anything wrong?"

"Martha? Did you hear?"

"No, I guess not. Hear what?"

"Lavender's been on the news. There was a shooting at the courthouse, and she was there."

"Oh, no! Is she alright?"

"Yes, she's fine. I'm sorry; I didn't mean to scare you. Lavender wasn't hurt, but she helped some woman who was shot by her husband. There was a child there, too, and Lavender was shown holding her. They were both all bloody."

"When did this happen? I can't believe she didn't even

call me," Martha said.

"Must have been this afternoon. She didn't call me, either. I guess she was too busy."

"It's hard to think of Lavender going through something like that and not getting in touch," Martha said. "I'm going to call her right now."

But Lavender's phone went straight to voice mail. Martha left a message: "Lavender, it's Martha. Aunt Pat just called, and told me you were involved in some kind of shooting today. She saw it on the news. Why didn't you call me? *Call* me!"

She went to bed when Zach did, but for a long time, she lay looking into the darkness.

CHAPTER TWENTY-ONE

2015

Lavender called her sister back first thing in the morning. She listened quietly to Martha's scolding without offering a defense. When Martha finally ran down, Lavender said, "I'm sorry you were worried and that you couldn't reach me last night. I'm perfectly fine today, but I've got a lot to do, so I'll have to cut this call short. Let's talk later, okay?"

She wasn't blowing Martha off; she really did have a big day ahead of her. In addition to the police interviews concerning what she saw and did when Rhonda was shot, there was Kaylie to consider. Arrangements must be made for her care while Rhonda was hospitalized. Lavender knew protocol dictated that the Department of Family and Children's Services take over and the child be placed in a temporary foster home, but she dreaded more changes for Kaylie. She called June for guidance.

"This case has been all over the news, so we can't fly under DFACS' radar," June said. "In fact, I've already gotten a call from a caseworker wanting to make arrangements to pick her up."

"But the poor little thing," Lavender said, "to have gone through what she did and then to be taken away from here, where she is at least familiar with her surroundings and knows some of us."

"I agree. I proposed that she be allowed to stay in our care until her mother is released. DFACS is thinking about it."

"It would just mean keeping her here and taking care of her as I've been doing until Rhonda is released, right?"

"That should be about it. Do you know if Rhonda has any relatives?"

"The only ones she mentioned to me were relatives of her husband. She was almost as afraid of them as of him."

"Let's make sure they don't get Kaylie, then. I'll work on it from this end. You concentrate on what the Nest needs this morning."

The Nest seemed to need quite a lot. One of the residents reported that the garbage disposal was jammed. Lavender found the instruction manual in the file. She discovered the little wrench taped to the unit, lay on her back, scooted under the sink and worked the wrench back and forth until the mechanism cleared. As she was rising triumphantly from that first-time-ever experience, bumping her head in the process, her cell phone rang. It was a police detective requesting that she come to the station for an interview. Then the newspaper called with the same request. Kaylie trailed into the kitchen dragging her blanket, wanting her Mommy, needing her face washed, and asking for breakfast.

Lavender looked around wildly. The urge to escape was strong. But there was a circle of women and children around her, upset by this latest evidence of the danger they were in themselves. Rhonda's shooting was a worst-case scenario that reminded each of them why they had abandoned their homes and fled to sanctuary. Now they looked to the safe house director – to Lavender – for reassurance. She took a deep breath and unclenched her hands.

"Let's have coffee, and talk," she said, sitting at the table, and hoisting Kaylie into her lap. The women scurried to fill cups. One of them filled a plate with cookies, and ushered the children into the playroom, Kaylie, too. This was a council of war, not a place for kids.

"We're all shaken by what happened to Rhonda," Lavender began. "Tell me what's going through your minds."

The voices collided and leapt over each other as the women expressed the fears they'd been harboring all night. What if? What then? Should I? Will he? Lavender listened.

"We're all safe here," she reminded them. "There's a policeman at the gate. Does anyone have to go out today?"

A hand rose. "I have a doctor appointment for Jaden to check on his ear infection."

"I'm supposed to meet with my social worker, but maybe I can reschedule. Or she could come here," another woman said.

"Anyone else? Okay, good. Those of you who don't have to go out, please stay put. I'll make a call and see about a police escort for Jaden's doctor appointment. Let's follow our usual schedule. Check the job sheet and do what you've signed up to do. Routine is our friend right now."

The woman scattered to their various duties, and Lavender dialed Mike's cell phone. He answered immediately.

"Lavender. I was hoping you'd call. Are you alright? I've been worried."

"I am, thanks. This is actually a business call. One of our residents has a doctor's appointment today, and we're concerned about her safety. Could you transport her?"

"Of course. It's my day off, but I'll take her myself."

~*~

Mike delivered his charges back to the Nest safely and accepted Lavender's invitation to come in for a minute. She'd just brewed a pot of coffee and poured two cups. The other women melted out of the kitchen with knowing smiles as Mike and Lavender sat down at the table.

"I'd like to see your new digs," Mike said.

"I'd like to show you, but oh my, what a lot of talk it would cause!" Lavender said, laughing.

"Have you had your police interview yet?" he asked.

"Yes, I went down to the station earlier today. They were very nice to me even though I couldn't be of much help because somehow I didn't see anything except Kaylie and Rhonda."

"You had tunnel vision. That's happened to me, too, in an emergency. Our field of vision narrows so we can see and hear only what we're focusing on. First responders learn to get over that."

"Mike, did I do the right thing? I can't remember what I did, to be honest."

"You slowed an arterial bleed until the EMTs got there. You probably saved Rhonda's life."

Mike's gaze was warm with admiration. Lavender felt compelled to be honest.

"I didn't think it through, I just acted. I'm surprised that I even know what a femoral artery is, let alone where it's located. My first class in CPR was only last week, and it sure didn't include that. I'm astonished that I was able to cope."

"Really?" Mike's surprise was unfeigned. "I've never seen you do anything *but* cope. And cope well."

"I'm flattered," Lavender said, "but it's not really me. I don't know what's happened to me lately."

"Well, don't worry about it," Mike advised. "Just go with it. If it sticks, then it's the new real you. Say, do you want to get some dinner tonight?"

"I'd love to, but not tonight. My residents are jumpy, and I promised them we'd have a movie and popcorn night."

"Sounds like fun. Room for one more?"

"Sorry, Mike, no men allowed. House rule."

"Some other time, then?"

"Definitely." She leaned full-length into his hug.

Martha left three messages before Lavender called her back. "Sorry," she said, "it's been a crazy day. I wonder if you'd have time to come to the Nest tomorrow and see my new quarters."

"I'd love to," Martha replied, "but I don't know where it is."

"Ah, good! Our strategy is working," Lavender said. "I'll pick you up at your house and drive you here, but then I'll have to kill you."

"Oh well, I've lived a rich, full life," Martha said. The sisters were laughing as they hung up.

Martha was lavish in her praise of Lavender's new room. "I love the way the light comes in the dormer windows," she said, "and look, there's the alphabet quilt. That makes it look like home. Your own bathroom! Where did you ever get that claw foot tub?"

"Believe it or not, it was in the basement, all covered in soot and home to a million spiders. I scrubbed and scrubbed, and then it took four of the construction crew to huff and puff it all the way up here. You should have seen them trying to get it around the bend at the landing. I had to make sure the kids were out of earshot so they didn't hear all the cussing."

"Well, it's perfect. I wish you many good long soaks in it. Are you happy here? Do you think you made a good choice in accepting this job?"

"I got off to such a dramatic start, it's hard to judge. But I think so. I've felt moments of panic when I realized how much people are counting on me. You know I've never been very reliable. Not even to myself."

"But we can change," Martha said earnestly. "I'm changing, too. Since that business with Kevin...Well, I'm in counseling trying to figure out what that showed me about myself."

"Really? I can't imagine you needing counseling. It was all my fault, anyway. I was the one who brought him into our lives. If I could pick Kevin, then I can't trust myself to make wise choices."

"My shrink says mistakes are opportunities to learn."

"Funny, that's what Aunt Pat says. And for free."

The alphabet quilt glowed in a sudden shaft of sunlight, catching their attention. "I wonder what Mom would think of all this," Lavender said.

"She wouldn't recognize you. Or me," Martha said.

"Do you think she'd be proud of us?"

"You know what? It doesn't matter anymore," Martha said. "Our job is to live our lives so we can be proud of ourselves."

CHAPTER TWENTY-TWO
2015

Kaylie was playing outside on the swing set with a couple of other kids, and Lavender was sitting in a lawn chair watching them. The sun warmed her body and the children's laughter warmed her heart. She leaned back and closed her eyes.

Gradually she became aware that the children's voices had taken on a different tone. Lavender roused herself. For a moment, she was sun-blind, but gradually she made out the figure of a man standing by the swings talking to the kids. As her eyes adjusted, she saw it was Kevin.

Leaping to her feet, she approached the group. "W-what are you d-doing here?" she demanded.

"Now just take it easy, you don't want to make a problem where there doesn't need to be one," Kevin said, watching her closely.

"It's a problem called t-trespassing," Lavender said. "How did you g-get in here? You n-need to leave now."

"Sure thing. How about I take this pretty little girl with me? You want to come with me, honey?" he asked Kaylie.

Kaylie's eyes darted to Lavender. With the intuition of children and animals, she knew this wasn't a good man, and he wasn't welcome here. She started to go to Lavender, but Kevin caught her, and lifted her into this arms.

"See, now, isn't this nice?" he said, his gaze never breaking Lavender's. "I'll just take this little cutie for some ice cream. You'd like that, wouldn't you, honey?"

"No! I wanna go to Miss Lavender."

"Yeah, lots of people do, lots of people do."

Kevin was walking rapidly toward the gate, ignoring Kaylie's flailing arms and legs. He'd be out on the sidewalk in a second; maybe he had a car waiting. Lavender couldn't stop to call for help. This was up to her.

She hit Kevin's back in a flying tackle, knocking him to the ground and sending Kaylie spurting out of his arms. Her wails filled the air and Lavender prayed the women in the house would hear and come to help. She drove her elbow into Kevin's kidney as he turned and threw her off.

She fell to the ground. Before she could regain her feet, he'd aimed a kick that caught her squarely in the midriff, sending a burst of pain through her ribs. In agony, she doubled up, gasping for air. The second kick caught her shoulder. When the third one came, she was ready. Grabbing Kevin's foot as it swung toward her, she pulled him off his feet. He landed with a yell as she threw herself on top of him.

Go for his eyes, she heard Mike say in her head, and she poked her thumbs into his eyeballs and gouged. He screamed, throwing up his arm to defend his face. Lavender reached under his arm and slashed the side of her hand against his windpipe. In her peripheral vision, she saw a gun on the ground. Her mind registered: *Pat's.* That was all she had time for.

She became aware that other hands were tearing at Kevin, other voices were raised in rage, and knew that her residents were fighting with her. The women piled on, sitting on his chest and legs, holding down his arms. Like Gulliver in the thrall of Lilliputians, Kevin was pinned to the ground. One of the women was on her cell phone, giving directions to the police. The children were being hustled back into the house by another mother. A third kicked the gun far away.

Lavender sat back on the grass, holding her ribs, trying to get a full breath. She was still trying when Mike and three other uniformed officers arrived, sirens blaring. Kevin was flipped over on his stomach, handcuffed with his hands behind his back, levered to his feet, and stuffed into a squad car. The gun was sealed into a plastic evidence bag. That was the last time Lavender saw it. Mike helped her to her feet, and held her shoulders when she suddenly doubled over to vomit.

"N-not my b-best look," she said ruefully when she'd finished.

"You look beautiful to me," Mike said, "and wow, you should see the other guy!"

~*~

"He must have seen Lavender on television," Martha said later to Pat. "We don't know how he found the Nest, but he did, and Mr. Techie that he is, he used some kind of electronic jamming device to prevent the gate from locking. All he had to do was push it open and he was in the grounds. The police think he's been there before, watching for a chance to get to Lavender."

"We should have killed him when we had the chance," Pat said disgustedly. "Now there's no telling what he'll say about us. The truth is bad enough, and no doubt he'll add lies."

"Does it matter?" Martha said. "He's in so much trouble himself, I don't think anyone will pay any attention to his tales. One thing, though. He had your gun with him."

"That means he was in your Mom's house. Lavender told me it was in the nightstand drawer in her room, and I've been meaning to go over and get it. Just never got around to it."

"You may be in trouble for not securing your firearm."

"Well, if I am, I deserve it. The gun is registered to me, and I have a permit for it, but it was careless of me to leave it in an empty house. Never too old to do something stupid, I always say. I'll just have to deal with whatever comes. The important thing is, how's Lavender?"

"She's got a broken rib but nothing can be done about it except tincture of time. Her stammer's back. You know how she gets when she's stressed. But her policeman friend, Mike, is being very supportive and her boss is, too. They realize that Lavender's had a horrendous start to her new job, and they've suggested she take a few days off. I think it's a good idea."

"Where will she go? Back to your Mom's house? I hope she knows she's always welcome here."

"She's welcome at my house, too, but I got the idea maybe she and Mike might be going somewhere. Together," Martha said.

"Is that a good idea?" Pat said. "Is she ready for a new relationship?"

"I don't know," Martha said. "I like Mike, but I'd hate to see her use another man to escape her troubles."

~*~

Lavender realized at a visceral level that she'd had

enough. The dream job had turned into a nightmare with two violent incidents occurring during her first week. While she felt she'd acquitted herself well both times, she was disheartened, exhausted, and in pain.

She took June up on her offer of time off, and retreated again to her mother's house to lick her wounds and think what to do next. Continuing as director at the Nest seemed impossible. Rhonda would soon be out of the hospital and she and Kaylie would move back into their home. Lavender was glad for them, but she had to admit that her most personally compelling reason for being at the Nest, Kaylie, would soon be gone. Now she had to figure out what to do with herself. But she was so sleepy. She spent long hours curled in her mother's bed.

When she was awake, she thought of Mike. There was definitely a spark between them. As far as she knew, he didn't have a wife and family lurking in the background. Was he Mr. Right, or just Mr. Right Now? No way to know. It was like walking around the store wearing the shoes you're thinking of buying. Sure, they feel fine, but you won't really know how they fit until you wear them for a day. Lavender called Mike and invited him to dinner. Time to try out those shoes.

He arrived right on time, carrying a big bouquet of supermarket roses. Lavender was ready. She'd reverted to full vamp mode: curled, creamed, scented, and brimming with charm. The smells from the kitchen alone might have been enough to win Mike's heart; throw in Lavender at her most appealing, and she figured he didn't stand a chance.

"Come in," she said, throwing open the door, her arms wide.

Mike looked faintly puzzled at her effusive welcome; she'd been much more low-key with him up to now. He returned her hug carefully, minding her broken rib, and gave her a peck on the cheek.

"Let me just put these beautiful flowers in water. Aren't you sweet to bring them. Come in, sit down. Dinner will be ready in a few minutes. Beer?"

When he was settled in the most comfortable chair, beer in hand, Lavender sat at his feet and looked up at him, turning on the full wattage of her amazing eyes. "Tell me about your day," she said.

"Well, let's see. Pretty ordinary, I guess," Mike said. "Stopped a few speeders in a school zone, gave a stranger-danger talk to first graders, and took a burglary report from one of the merchants on the square. Nothing very exciting. What about you? How was your day?"

"Quiet," Lavender said, biting her lip, and dropping her gaze. "I'm sort of lost right now. When I close my eyes, I see Kevin grabbing Kaylie."

"Yeah, that was rough. But you swung right into action. Those self-defense classes really paid off, huh?"

"I didn't even think; I just did it."

"No higher praise than that. When your moves become instinctive, then you know you've got it."

"But..."

"I'm proud of you, Lavender. You showed you can react in an emergency. Do you know how rare that is? Most people either freeze or panic. Not you."

"But, you see, that's not really me. I, uh, I prefer an easier life."

"Don't we all? But being able to handle tough situations, that's the mark of a competent person. Mmmm, what's that good smell? I'm starved."

"Well, then let's eat," Lavender said, and led the way to the dining room. Maybe this was going to take a little longer than she'd thought. They settled back in the living room with glasses of wine after dinner.

"When are you going back to work?" Mike asked.

"I'm not sure. I'm kind of rethinking right now. Maybe I won't go back to the Nest. Maybe it's not the right place for me after all."

"Are you kidding?" Mike said. "I think it's the perfect place for you, and you just proved it. Why wouldn't you return?"

"Maybe I need a change. You know, I've been volunteering there for several months."

"I've been a cop for ten years, the last three of them on the same beat. My dad worked at his job for thirty years. I think there's a lot of value in perseverance."

"Yes, there's something in what you say. But I'm..."

"You don't just cut and run when the going gets rough. Do you?"

"No, no, of course not. I guess I just need some time."

"Get right back on the horse that threw you," Mike advised briefly. He didn't look enchanted with her. He looked disappointed.

CHAPTER TWENTY-THREE

2015

Pat was not having a happy time. The magistrate judge glared at her over the tall bench and pulled no punches.

"You ought to know there are laws about unsecured guns. If a minor had gotten access to your firearm and harmed himself or someone else, you might well be heading to jail right now. As it is, your gun ended up in a safe house for victims of violence. How do you think those mothers felt, seeing a gun on the grounds of their sanctuary? They and their children may have faced gun violence before; that may have been why they fled their homes. Then, thanks to your neglect, a gun threatened them again in the place where they should have been able to feel safe."

"Your Honor, I have no excuse. It was pure carelessness on my part," Pat said.

"I see you have a permit for the gun and had military training in firearms. That you're a veteran works in your favor," the judge said, slightly mollified by Pat's obvious contrition. "I believe that you didn't intend to endanger anyone. However, you and I both know what road is paved with good intentions. You might consider getting one of the new smart guns that requires fingerprint recognition before it can be fired. I'm going to dismiss your case with a warning that if I ever see or hear of you being in trouble because of a firearm again, I'll bring the full force of the law down upon you."

"Thank you, Your Honor," Pat said. She escaped into the sunlight with mixed feelings of relief and shame. How would she ever make it up to Lavender for worsening an already bad situation? She had to see her right away to apologize again.

Lavender opened the door still in her pajamas, although it was almost noon.

"Oh, hi, Aunt Pat," she said, with a yawn. "What brings you here so early?"

"Well, first of all, it isn't early, it's noon. Second, I just came from the worst scolding I've ever gotten in my life, and I totally deserved it. I'm here to say again how sorry I am that I left my gun where Kevin could get hold of it. It makes me sick to think of what could have happened."

"But it didn't happen, so stop beating yourself up. Remember, I'm the one who brought Kevin into your life, so if you want to talk about blame..."

"Maybe we'd better just take a break from discussing the whole Kevin thing," Pat said. "There's plenty of blame to go around where he's concerned. What are you doing with yourself these days?"

"Oh, nothing much. Waiting for my rib to heal. Sleeping a lot," Lavender said.

"Why are you so sleepy? Are you depressed?" Pat asked bluntly.

177

"I don't know, maybe. My life has fallen apart. Again."

"You certainly went through some back-to-back traumas, but I wouldn't say your life has fallen apart. You still have your job and your health," Pat said.

"Yeah. I guess. But I don't think I want to go back to the Nest. It's too hard. I'm not cut out for it."

"Oh, Lavender, what nonsense. Think of what you've handled: Kevin's stalking and injury, Rhonda's shooting, and the aftermath, and Kevin trying to abduct Kaylie. Why, it sounds like a bad afternoon soap. But you came through in every situation and did yourself proud."

"Yes, but that doesn't feel like me. What feels like me is to get the heck out of all this mess and find an easier life."

Pat looked at her thoughtfully for a moment before she spoke. "Look, you know I'm not long on tact, so I'm just going to come out with it. Your mother and Martha meant the best in the world for you, but what they actually did was enable you to get away with sliding through life. Your beauty made men want to rescue you, and you allowed that to happen. Inside, I believe there is a strong woman who can rise to any occasion. We've watched her in action lately. Now I'm seeing the passive, helpless girl again, but I think she's only here because you're tired and worn out."

"Is that Pop Psychology 101?" Lavender asked angrily.

"Nope, just your old Aunt Pat spouting off. But I've watched you grow up, child. I know you as well as anybody. I believe in you. You can change the way you go through this world. Martha is changing, and by golly, I'm going to make some changes, too."

~*~

Mike didn't call the next day as Lavender expected.

Every other man had called promptly after being exposed to the full Lavender whammy. What made this one different? She felt a little stirring of challenge. She called him.

"Oh, hi, I'm pretty busy right now," he said. "Meet you for lunch? Sure, I should be able to get away about 11:30."

They settled into the diner's padded red booth and ordered BLTs and Cokes. Lavender tried again. She lowered her head and looked at Mike from under her lashes. He didn't seem to notice as he unwrapped his silverware and spread the napkin in his lap.

"Do you ever feel like just running away?" she asked.

"Who doesn't?" Mike grinned good-naturedly.

"Lately, that's what I've felt like doing," she continued. "Just taking off for someplace warm, with a beach. Spending some time soaking up sun and Margaritas."

"Yeah, sounds nice."

"Do you think so? We could do it, you know. Just take off."

"Uh huh."

"No, I mean it. We could leave today."

"You're kidding, right? I've got a job, you've got a job, and neither of us has that kind of money. Besides, is that where we are in our relationship? Are we even *in* a relationship?"

Lavender wasn't used to such straight talk from a man upon whom she'd set her sights. She blinked in surprise. "I thought – I th-thought you wanted to be," she said.

"You're a gorgeous woman," Mike said. "Any man would want to date you. You're beautiful and glamorous and fun. But what I'm looking for at this point in my life is something more serious than a good time. I'm thirty-seven. I want a wife, a home and kids. Frankly, I don't have time to waste on party girls."

"Is th-that what you think I am?"

"I don't know. I didn't think so at first, but...Well, we're still getting to know each other."

Lavender's cheeks burned with embarrassment and anger. "I've b-been through some things lately..."

"You have. And you've handled yourself like a champ. Maybe you just need some time to process everything. I'd say about the last thing you need is to complicate your life by rushing into a relationship - with me or anyone else."

"You seem to have me all f-figured out," she said. "What else do I need to d-do?"

"Look, don't get mad. I just think it's important to start out the way we mean to go on, if we do go on. I'm being totally honest, and I mean that as a compliment to you. No games, no hide and seek. I want an equal partner for life, a strong woman who can support me when I need it, and who lets me support her. I'm ready to settle down. Maybe it's what you want, maybe not, but it's good to get it straight up front."

"I don't think it *is* what I w-want," Lavender said, "b-but thanks for the free advice." She rose, grabbed her purse, and walked out the door.

~*~

I'm not the most articulate guy in the world, Lavender read, *and I guess I made a mess of what I said today at lunch. I do care for you, and I'd like for us to see if we might have a future together. But I meant it when I said it's better to get everything straight from the get-go. To me, that means taking our time, and really getting to know each other in the most honest way. If I hurt your feelings, I'm sorry. You may be mad at me for being so frank, but I hope when you've thought things over, you'll agree. What do you want in life, Lavender? What are your goals and hopes and dreams? Until you know that, you can't know anything else."*

Blast the man! Lavender crumpled his letter in her hand but she refrained from pitching into the wastebasket. The note had apparently been slipped under the door while she was in the back yard, taking out her frustrations by viciously weeding her mother's wildflower garden. She'd found it just now when she came in for a drink of water, and picked it up with her earth-stained hands.

She sat at the kitchen table, smoothed out the note, and read it again. What *did* she want in life? Did she, in fact, have any goals or dream?. *What he's really saying is that I bring nothing to the table,* she thought. *I'm just another pretty face, and even that won't last forever. He wants more than that, and I can't blame him.*

She spent the rest of the evening deep in thought, and that night she had a dream. It was a restless, disjointed kind of dream, one that made little sense. She was in a car that alternately sped and stalled. She seemed to be in the back seat when it was speeding, with no one at the wheel. In terror, she realized she was supposed to be driving. Then the car stalled. She got out and pushed with all her strength but couldn't budge it one inch. Finally, she climbed into the driver's seat, revved the engine, and...woke up.

She knew better than to tell Martha her dreams, but as the day wore on she couldn't shake the restless, unsettled feelings this one had given her. Finally, she called Pat.

"Huh. Well, I guess the car could represent your journey through life," Pat said thoughtfully. "When it sped up with nobody driving, it might mean you aren't taking control. When it stalled, you couldn't get it going until you got behind the wheel – took charge. But then you woke up, so we don't know how it ended."

"I think I do know, though, Aunt Pat," Lavender said. "I think I do know."

~*~

Lavender went back to work. At the end of her week off, she simply packed her suitcase and drove back to the Nest. The women and children greeted her happily, eager to talk about the excitement of Kevin's apprehension. Rhonda had been released from the hospital that morning, and she and Kaylie were spending their last night at the Nest. The next day they'd be moving home. Already, Lavender could see a difference in them. Their new self-confidence was beautiful.

She excused herself after a few minutes and headed up to her attic hideaway. In the peaceful room, the alphabet quilt murmured stories of long-ago women who had stitched its patterns. The blocks that she and Pat made were the newest and brightest; in time, they would fade to match the others. Her mother had worked on the quilt, too, Lavender was sure of it, but she'd never know the story behind it. For a moment, she missed her mother fiercely. She was proud to belong to this line of women who'd stitched their lives into patterns for future generations.

Her thoughts turned to Mike. Would he be glad she'd returned to work? She wasn't doing it for his approval; she needed to stay this course for her own sake. Mike had been honest about what kind of woman he wanted in his life. Maybe she could be that person, but first she'd prove it to herself. To be independent, to do worthwhile work, to stop running and learn how to rescue herself – those were her goals. As for Mike, they would either connect as equals or not at all. When she didn't need him anymore, then she'd see if she still wanted him.

CHAPTER TWENTY-FOUR
2016

Martha couldn't figure out why her mornings had taken such a bad turn. Rising with a churning stomach, unable to drink coffee, feeling generally crummy – that just wasn't her. She usually sprang from bed filled with crackling energy. She wondered if she was still depressed, despite her continuing productive sessions with Dr. Bachmann. She discussed it with Zach.

"Maybe you're just a little run down," he suggested absently, not looking up from his newspaper. "Before you blame it on depression, why don't you get a physical? You might need vitamins or something."

So Martha presented herself to their long-time family doctor and submitted to an examination. She was unprepared for his findings.

"I'm going to refer you to your OB/GYN for further tests," the doctor said. He smiled. "I think what ails you is out of my field of expertise."

"What is it?" Martha asked, alarmed. "Do you think I

have cancer or something?"

"No, no, nothing like that. I'm seeing some signs that may be early menopause, or --"

"Or what?"

"Or maybe pregnancy. But like I said, that's not my field."

Martha went straight to a drugstore and bought a pregnancy test kit. In the privacy of her own bathroom she followed the directions, and with shaking hands, examined the dipstick. Sure enough, it changed color. She sat down hard on the side of the tub. Pregnant! At her age! The boys were in their teens. What would they say about having a new sibling so much younger than they? And Zach. How would he take to starting over with diapers and night feedings at their stage of life?

True, she and Zach had been experiencing a new closeness since she'd opened her heart to him. His initial anger had given way to an intimacy in which they shared their thoughts and feelings as they had done not in years. *Oh, boy, did we share!* Martha thought. She decided to keep this knowledge to herself for a few days until she'd had time to assimilate it.

Maybe it would be a girl this time. At forty-three, she wasn't impossibly old to be having a baby. Lots of women deferred childbirth until their late thirties; and besides, she'd already given birth twice, so her body knew how to do it. Martha began to feel some stirrings of excitement. She could do over the spare room in an orgy of pink, buy those adorable little outfits with rosebud prints. There'd be future ballet lessons and tea parties – tutus and teacups instead of soccer cleats and sweatshirts. This could be fun.

Now if only Zach shared her optimism. She wouldn't

know until she told him. Maybe tonight, on their evening walk.

~*~

The sisters sat at Martha's kitchen table having tea. Lavender noted, and wondered, about Martha's pallor, which didn't exactly correspond to the gleam in her eye. Something was up, but she decided to let Martha tell her in her own time. It didn't take long.

"So," Martha began, leaning forward with an air of importance. "I have something to tell you."

"I gathered. What's going on? I hope it's good news," Lavender said.

"We think so," Martha said, her grin stretching from ear to ear. "You're going to be an aunt – again."

"Martha! You're having a baby? That's wonderful. How did – well, I know how it happened, but how long have you known? What did Zach say? What did the boys say? How do you feel? How far along are you? Oh, my gosh, a new baby – at *your* age!"

"Zach was shocked, of course, as I was. But the more we talked about it, the more it began to seem like an adventure. We're not that old, you know. It's not like people will mistake us for the baby's grandparents."

"Of course they won't. This baby will keep you young for years. What about the boys? Are they thrilled at the prospect of a new sibling?"

"I wouldn't say thrilled, exactly. Embarrassed is more like it. Proof that their parents have sex was almost more than their little teenage hearts could take. But they'll get used to the idea."

"Are you going to find out beforehand if it's a girl or a boy? I hope you will, it will make shopping so much easier."

"You betcha. We both want to know for sure, but Lavender, I just know it's a girl this time. I'm trying not to get my hopes up too much, but somehow I feel I know. Her name is Grace."

~*~

Pat shook open three big, black trash bags. One for discards, one for donations, and one for keeping. She eyed the piles of stuff, then set the kitchen timer for thirty minutes. Resolutely focusing on one small section of her dining room, she began. Sometimes an item made her pause for long moments of thought before she was able to choose which bag to put it in. When the timer rang, the donations bag was half full, the discard bag contained only a few things, and the keep bag was bulging.

"This is harder than it looks," she said aloud.

~*~

Lavender and Mike had a more or less standing date every Saturday night. Lavender had a dependable volunteer on that night, and Mike was on day watch, so it worked out for them. Movies, casual dinners, walks in good weather, a few times they rented a rowboat and rowed around the little lake in the park. Their evenings were not exciting, but she looked forward to them all week. Talking with Mike was far-ranging and easy. Lavender felt she knew him as well as she'd ever known anyone. In turn, she confided in him things she'd never verbalized: her reliance on one man after another to fix her life, her dependence on, and resentment of Martha, her fear that, now that her mother was gone, she was adrift in a world that wouldn't always favor her. He never said much to these confessions, just nodded, and sometimes put his arm around her and squeezed briefly. When she asked his advice, he usually said, "I know you can figure it out. You're one of the most competent people I know."

Not a lot of sparks flew when they were together, but a steady warmth emanated from Mike and she basked in it. As for his belief in her competency, she turned that over and over in her mind. It didn't fit her picture of herself, but maybe, just maybe she was changing.

No more extreme dramas interrupted the days at the Nest. Women came and went, some with their faces swollen like failed pugilists, some angry and bitter, some so afraid they could hardly speak above a whisper. Kaylie and Rhonda were well established back in their home, and Lavender visited them there a couple of times. At the Nest, she took care to keep a little bit of herself in reserve, realizing the truth of June's warning about burning out.

News of Martha's pregnancy filled her with delight and a new emotion. Envy. Lavender wished she were having that baby. A little niece named Grace would be wonderful, of course, but she wanted her own child. She told Martha so.

"Well, nothing's stopping you," Martha said. "I'm sure Mike would be glad to oblige."

"Not unless he puts a ring on it," Lavender said with a rueful laugh. "He's old school. First a wedding, then a house in the 'burbs, then, in due time, parenthood."

"So, what's wrong with that?"

"Nothing. Nothing. It's just...so permanent."

"You know the cliché; life is what happens while we're making other plans," Martha said. "Or in your case, making no plans at all. You're not getting any younger, you know. If you really want a child, you need to get going."

"But do you think I could be a good wife and mother? I've been – well, maybe a little flighty all my life."

"Yeah, I noticed that," Martha said. "Of course you

would be a good wife and mother. Didn't we have one of the best to pattern ourselves after? All you have to do is commit."

"And that's the hard part," Lavender said.

~*~

Martha's pregnancy was going well. After she got over the initial morning sickness, she felt fine. Her obstetrician was pleased. Zach was increasingly enthusiastic, and even the boys showed some signs of interest in a new sibling.

"Grace, huh?" one of them said, "Like for Grandma?"

"Yes, for Grandma," Martha replied. "Don't you think it's a good way to honor Grandma and remember her, to name the new baby after her?"

"I guess. Will we have to baby-sit?"

"Probably. This is your sister, after all. We're all responsible for each other in this family, and we help each other out, right?"

Martha had an ultra-sound, which confirmed her already-certain knowledge that she was carrying a girl. The nursery was painted the palest of pinks, and the alphabet quilt was folded over the end of the crib. Lavender and Pat had already produced such a blizzard of girly baby-clothes that Martha finally begged them to stop on the grounds that no baby could wear all that gear before she outgrew it.

"No worries," Lavender responded, "when Gracie outgrows something, I'll take it to the Nest. We always need kids' clothes there."

Martha loved the confidence with which Lavender spoke of the Nest and her job there. She'd almost completed her first year and showed no signs of wanting to move on. After her rocky start, Martha feared Lavender would follow her usual pattern and cut and run, but she'd shown admirable perseverance. She looked for signs that her sister's new-found maturity would spill over into her relationship with Mike. The old Martha would have been scolding, advising and exhorting Lavender to grab her chance. The new Martha let her be.

CHAPTER TWENTY-FIVE

2016

"We've gotten an offer on the house," Martha said into the phone.

"Really? Is it a good one?" Lavender asked.

"Asking price. For some reason, the buyer wants to take it as is, with all the household stuff, china, linen and furniture still in there. He did ask that Mom's clothes and toiletries be removed."

"Oh, I hate to let her things go," Lavender said.

"Yeah, well, you had your chance to clear them out, but you didn't get it done, so now you don't get to complain."

"You're right, you're right. I'll run over whenever I have an hour or two to spare and pack up her clothes. Can we take mementos, do you think?"

"I'm not sure. We'll have to ask the buyer, I guess. Why, what do you want?"

"Just a place setting of her everyday dishes. They say

'home' to me. And maybe that little demi lune table in the foyer." Lavender said. "Don't you want a keepsake?"

"I like the idea of a place setting, only I'd like to have one in her good china. Just to put in my sideboard. You're right; those dishes are so evocative of her. I don't want any furniture, though," Martha said. "My house is full."

In the weeks between the offer and closing, the sisters gradually packed up their mother's personal items. Everything else, they left in place. It was strange to think of those familiar objects being used by a stranger, but they reminded each other that life is all about changes, and this one was long overdue. They were curious about what buyer would want to step into someone else's possessions.

Martha received a phone call that cleared it up. "Mike?" she said. "Is everything okay? Why are you calling?"

"Everything's fine. I want to tell you something, but please promise me you won't tell Lavender."

"Okay, shoot."

"I'm the buyer. I'm the guy who's buying your mom's house."

"You? Why? What do you want with our house – and all Mom's stuff?"

"I've been saving for a house for a long time. This one is in a great neighborhood with a good school within walking distance. And it's just the kind of house I like, especially with all the quirky doo-dads and add-ons your Dad did."

"But...our house! I don't know what to say."

"Say you won't tell Lavender," Mike pleaded.

"No, I won't, but she'll find out. Won't she have to sign the papers at closing, along with me?"

"Is there any way we could work around that?" Mike asked. "If the realtor can figure out a way to get her signature at another time, or you could get her Power of Attorney and sign for her, would you be willing to do it?

"You're going to have to give me a darn good reason to deceive my sister," Martha said sternly.

"Okay, here's the thing. I'm hoping that house will become the home of Lavender and Mike Olsen. I know she loves it, and the furnishings have a lot of sentimental value to her. I want to surprise her with it when I ask her to marry me. Kind of sweeten the deal, you know?"

"I wondered if you were ever going to get around to proposing. I don't know what she'll say but you can be sure if she says yes, it will be because she loves you, house or no house."

"Do you think she will? Say yes?" Mike sounded very young, and uncertain.

"I wouldn't dare predict Lavender's behavior. She seems more grown-up and settled, but there's no telling whether she's ready to make a commitment. That's been hard for her all her life. I can only wish you well. I think marrying you would be absolutely the best thing in the world for Lavender."

Martha struggled with herself for a moment. Then she continued, "Forgive me for asking this, but I feel I must. Are you sure marrying Lavender would be the best thing in the world for you?"

"What do you mean?"

"She's my sister and I love her dearly, but I think there are some things about her that will never change."

"I'm counting on that," Mike said. "Her sweetness, her

beauty, her sense of humor..."

"All great qualities, but are you prepared to deal with her vagueness about money? She's not a spendthrift, but she's impractical about keeping track of expenses and paying bills."

"We've talked about that. She's trying to do better, but I know what you mean: it's a trait that's probably not going to change after – if – we're married. I can deal with it. I'm a whiz-bang at managing money, and she's more than willing to let somebody else do it for her."

"There have been a lot of boyfriends," Martha said hesitantly.

"I know about them," Mike said. "Can't say I'm thrilled, but that was before we met. What's important is what happens now. Anything else you want to warn me about?"

"A while ago, I would have said irresponsibility, passiveness and laziness, but I've seen her make such changes," Martha said. She paused, then added, "I hope you know I love Lavender, and I'm talking to you like this only because I want you both to be happy."

"I know that, and I appreciate your honesty. I'm not perfect, either. I might just have one or two tiny little faults that will drive Lavender crazy. She says I'm a young guy with an old man's outlook on life, while she's a free spirit. But don't worry about us. We both have our eyes wide open."

~*~

Martha's back ached. No matter how she positioned herself, the niggling pain persisted. "Too early for labor," she told herself and Zach. "I must have slept wrong or twisted or something." She paused frequently to stretch with her hands on her lower back, and eventually the pain subsided.

Today, Friday, was closing day for Mike's purchase of

the family home. Lavender was still completely in the dark as to the identity of the buyer, and Martha had bitten her tongue more times than she cared to remember. It seemed like too big a surprise to spring on anyone – a marriage proposal, and, hey, the house comes with it. But she'd promised Mike, so she kept quiet.

The realtor was in on the deception and assured Martha that, as executor of her mother's will, she could finalize the sale papers alone. Lavender was relieved. "I don't want to be there," she told Martha. "I just want to remember the house the way it was when we grew up. If I don't take part in the sale, I can pretend it's still there, intact."

Little do you know how intact! Martha thought.

The closing went off without a hitch. Mike's finances were in admirable shape. Martha was impressed that he'd saved so much money on a policeman's salary. When she asked him how he'd done it, he said it was years of frugal living in tiny apartments. "No bar-hopping with the guys after work or big nights on the town," he said. "I drive an old beater and haven't taken a real vacation in – I don't know when. But it's been totally worth it, because now I've got this great house."

She already liked Mike, and now his enthusiasm for her childhood home endeared him to her still more. Lavender would be nuts to pass this guy up, but she'd been doing nutty things all her life. She discussed it with Zach, who said he could only hope. "Somebody else to write the checks when she comes up short," he sighed. "What bliss."

"But she hasn't asked you to cover for her lately, has she?" Martha asked.

"Not since she went back to the Nest last summer, and now it's almost Christmas. I guess her job keeps her so busy she doesn't have time to spend money."

"Or much need to, since she let her apartment go, and lives expense-free. She's dating only Mike, and their idea of a big night is a walk in the park. Oh, I hope this works out for her! Mike is pure gold. I think they could be so happy."

"Sweetie, let it be," Zach said gently.

Martha laughed at herself. "You're right. I've got all I can carry – literally."

~*~

Mike picked Lavender up at the usual time on Saturday evening. They went to their favorite diner and had their favorite meal, cheeseburgers and chocolate milkshakes.

"I'm a lucky guy that you don't want to go someplace fancy," he told her.

"Been there, done that," she said. "There's a lot to be said for the simple life. And, by the way, my treat tonight. You've paid the last couple of times."

"Ah, I see the method in your frugal madness now," Mike said, "but it's okay, I'm a cheap date."

After dinner, he drove toward the house, refusing to answer Lavender's questions about where they were going. As they turned down the familiar street, Lavender said, "Oh, no, Mike, I don't want to see the house. Someone else owns it now, and I just want to remember it when it was ours."

"One last look, honey," Mike said.

He watched her eyes widen when she saw every window was illuminated by a tiny candle on the sill. "Oh," she breathed. "How pretty it looks. No, don't drive in."

But Mike switched off the car in the driveway and came around to open Lavender's door. She looked up at him in bewilderment.

"Do you know the people who bought it?" she asked.

"Yes, and so do you. Come on, we're expected."

When he produced the key to the front door, she looked at him searchingly. He ushered her inside to the living room lit by a glowing Christmas tree. Groups of candles flickered, and the clean scent of pine filled the air. Lavender's glance took in the familiar furnishings. Two glasses of wine waited on the coffee table. Mike picked them up and handed one to her.

"Here's to new life in an old house," he said, his voice breaking a little.

"Mike, tell me this instant what is going on."

He set down his wineglass, reached into his pocket, and produced an unmistakable jeweler's box. "Lavender," he said, "I love you, and I want you to be my wife. I hope we'll live together in this house and raise a family of our own. Will you marry me?"

He flicked open the box, and Lavender saw a small emerald-cut diamond solitaire winking back at her. For a moment, she couldn't speak.

"*You* are the buyer? You bought the house for me – for us?"

"Yes. I know you love it."

There was a long pause. Lavender walked slowly around the room. She plumped up a pillow on the sofa and straightened a drapery. "You went to a lot of trouble," she murmured. He waited, his face reflecting his anxiety.

Finally, she spoke. "I'm touched beyond what I can express that you'd do this for me. To continue the life of our family in this house - my Mom and Dad would be so thrilled."

"So it's yes?" Mike didn't want to leave anything up in the air.

"But I come with some baggage, you know, big trunks of it. My past hasn't been exactly blameless. In fact, some things happened in this very house that I've never told you about. How can you be sure I won't revert to my old ways? I'm not even sure myself, some days."

"Whatever your experiences have been, they all made you the person you are today, the woman I love," Mike said. "I have no concern that you'll revert, as you call it, because I've watched you grow and change for the past year. I trust you with my life."

Lavender's beautiful eyes filled with tears. She returned to Mike's side and took both his hands in hers. "Then yes!" she said, "I will marry you and we'll live in this house and make a life and a family together. I promise."

Mike took the ring from the box and slipped it on Lavender's finger. They were admiring the way the diamond caught the light when Martha's voice broke the spell.

"Is it safe to come out now?" she called.

"Martha? What are you doing here?" Lavender said.

"Somebody had to tend to these candles and make sure the new owner didn't burn his house down before he ever moved in," Martha said, as she and Pat emerged, laughing, from the bedroom where they'd been hiding.

"For heaven's sake, Mike!" Lavender said, but she was laughing, too. "Why not just invite the whole street to our most intimate moment?"

"I know the McGuire girls stick together through everything," Mike said, "so I figured it was just a matter of time until they were here with us anyway."

At that moment, Martha gasped, and they all followed the direction of her gaze to the spreading puddle at her feet.

"Oh, my gosh, my water just broke," she said. "It's not time yet."

"Quick, sit down, no, lie down. Let's get her to the car. Should I call 911? Where's my phone? I'll call Zach," Lavender said, in a flurry of panicky activity.

But Martha was doubled over, helpless with pain. Pat and Mike exchanged a look, and then Mike moved calmly to Martha's side as Pat disappeared in the direction of the bedroom.

"Come along, Martha," Mike said, supporting her as he steered her gently after Pat. The bed was padded thickly with towels by the time they got there, and Martha was helped to lie down.

"I can't wait," she wailed, "the baby's coming right now."

"It's okay, you've got a paramedic and a nurse beside you," Pat said. "We've done this before and so have you. Relax between the pains if you can. We've got you."

But there wasn't time to relax. In a matter of moments, with a shout of triumph, Martha announced the arrival in the world of her daughter.

When the paramedics got there, the cord was cut, the baby swaddled, and mother and child were loaded onto a stretcher for the trip to the hospital. Lavender climbed into the back of the ambulance with her sister.

"I'm going," she said flatly to the medic, who would have preferred to have her work space clear of superfluous persons. And so the McGuire sisters, plus one, rode to the hospital, where Zach paced in the ambulance bay waiting for them. Mother and baby were wheeled into an examination room where the obstetrician on call saw them.

"A healthy baby girl," she pronounced. "Good set of lungs, just a tad under six pounds and very unusual color eyes."

Lavender winked at Martha. "Maybe they'll change color as she gets older," she said.

"Is she okay, though?" Zach asked nervously. "To come so fast, and before the due date even..."

"Babies who are born in a rush like this are usually so healthy all anyone has to do is catch them so they don't fall on the floor," the doctor said. "Congratulations, Mom and Dad. You've got a beautiful baby."

CHAPTER TWENTY-SIX

2017

"Their wedding was exactly right for them," Martha said, as she toed off her high-heels with a sigh of relief.

She, Zach and the boys had just returned from Mike and Lavender's nuptials, held in what was now their home. Martha sat for a moment and reviewed the day while Zach paid the baby-sitter.

Lavender and Mike's plan to say their vows beneath the blooming Japanese cherry tree in the back yard was thwarted when gray April rain clouds chose to shed their burden five minutes before the wedding. Plan B was to hold the ceremony in the central hall of the house. The irony of it taking place on the same spot where Kevin had sprawled was not lost on Lavender, Martha and Pat. But it wasn't a time to focus on difficult memories. Lavender was radiant in a pale lilac dress. Mike's face shone with such love that it had their little assembly dabbing their eyes. Vows were spoken firmly and clearly. This was a couple who knew exactly what they were doing.

After the brief ceremony, the family gathered in the dining room for Champagne and wedding cake. Pat had done herself proud with the cake she insisted on baking. It was a confection of strawberries, flowers and butter-crème frosting. When everyone had a slice, and all the wine glasses were filled, she stood and waited until she had everyone's attention.

"As the oldest family member, it falls to me to make a toast," she said. "Here's to Lavender and Mike. May you live in this house as happily as Grace and Tommy did." She paused for a moment to swallow hard and regain her composure; then she continued. "If your Mom and Dad could see you today – well, maybe they can, who knows? – they'd be proud and happy. Just as we all are."

Glasses were raised and clinked together. "Hear, hear! To Lavender and Mike."

Simple, intimate and elegant. It had been a most satisfactory wedding, Martha reflected. She thought about the direction their lives had taken during the past year. Gracie was five months old and thriving. The baby had slipped seamlessly into their lives, making willing slaves of them all. She'd inherited the recessive gene that produced eyes so blue they looked almost purple. Sometimes, when Gracie gave her a certain look, Martha had a dizzy feeling of déjà vu.

Pat had actually cleaned her house. It still wasn't a candidate for *House Beautiful*, but it was fairly tidy and loosely organized. Pat said she didn't know why she'd hung on to all that old junk for so long.

And Lavender: a married woman now, ensconced in her beloved childhood home, still working at the Nest, pursuing a degree in social work through evening classes. Who could have predicted that soft-focus, dreamy Lavender would transform herself into a woman of purpose?

Martha's reverie was broken when she heard Gracie tuning up in the nursery. She rose to her feet. "Coming," she called. For a moment, she felt her own mother's presence.

AFTERWORD

On a sunny July afternoon, Martha dropped Gracie off at Lavender's while she ran errands. The baby dozed in her stroller in the shade while Lavender got back to weeding. Her mother and father had created a little slice of paradise in their backyard and Lavender and Mike tended it faithfully. When Martha returned, Lavender took her on an inspection tour.

"I love the arbor Mike built," Martha said. "And you've got the grass looking great. Dad would be pleased. But what have you done with the wildflower garden?" Martha asked, when they came to a bare space.

"Mike dug it up," Lavender said. "Some of those plants were poisonous, you know. Remember how ferociously Mom warned us not to pick the wild flowers? I never understood why she was so adamant about keeping them, anyway."

"They must have had some special meaning to her. We'll never know."

"But we do know she'd have wanted the babies to be safe."

Martha turned to her sister joyfully. "Babies, plural? You mean you're…?"

"Yes. We just found out yesterday," Lavender said. "It's early, but the doctor says I'm healthy as a brood-mare – that's the term he used – and shouldn't have any trouble. Since I'm thirty-nine, and Mike is thirty-eight, we don't have any time to waste. When this one's born, we'll have a second child as soon as possible. It'll be chaos, but then we'll have our family."

They regarded Gracie, awake now and clamoring for freedom. Once out of her stroller, she squirmed to be put down on the green grass, crawling away as fast as her chubby knees would take her.

"Mike says I'm getting broody," Lavender said. "But he's just as bad - nesting and all that. We can't stop cleaning and organizing. He's working in the attic and my next project is sorting Mom's books. Will you take a look and see if there's anything you want?"

"Sure. I'll come back later, after Zach gets home and can watch the baby."

~*~

"Hey, Lavender, what do you want me to do with this old trunk?"

Mike's voice floated down from the attic. The sisters were sorting books in the wide central hallway. They glanced up at the ceiling, as if expecting guidance from their dead mother.

"Bring it down, and we'll figure it out," Lavender called back.

They heard the trunk scraping across the plywood of the attic's floor, accompanied by Mike's grunts of exertion, and a few choice words.

"It weighs a dang ton. Better get back and give me plenty of room," he said, as the edge of the trunk emerged in the opening of the trapdoor.

"Look out!" Mike yelled a second later. The trunk teetered, lost its fight with gravity and crashed downward, clipping the bookcase. It landed with a shattering crash. Mike's face appeared in the opening. He scanned the sisters to make sure they were unhurt. "Oops," he said.

The trunk, now in several pieces, littered the floor. Mike scrambled down and they surveyed the wreckage in silence.

"I hope there wasn't too much sentimental value there," he said.

"No, not really," Lavender replied. "It was just an old trunk that had been around forever. Mom said it was in her room when she was growing up, used to store odds and ends. I don't know why she kept it all those years."

"Look," Martha said. She'd squatted down to examine a small book half-covered by the rubble. "I think this is a diary. See, it's got a little lock. I wonder whose it was. I didn't see it when I cleaned out the trunk earlier."

Mike bent down beside her and stirred around in the trunk's pieces. "Looks like the trunk had a false bottom," he said. "Somebody must have hidden the diary there. We'd never have found it if I hadn't dropped the damn thing."

"Let's see if we can figure out who it belonged to," Lavender said.

"It's locked," Martha said.

"Not anymore," Mike said, snapping the brittle old lock with one tug.

The book fell open with a little puff of dust. Yellowed

pages were divided into days of the week. Faded, childish handwriting on the first page identified the owner as Grace Strunk.

"It's Mom's!" Martha said.

"I'll leave you to it," Mike said, "I've got some more stuff to bring down."

The sisters' heads bent over the old book as they read the entries penned by their mother long ago.

January 1, 1962 - This is my new diary Janice gave me for my birthday. I waited until the New Year to start, and now I'm going to write in it every day. I'll hide it from Mother so I can say whatever I want to. I hope I'll have some good things to write.

*****

February 4, 1962 - Mother tore up all my paper dolls today because I played with them when I was supposed to be dusting. I cried, and then she spanked me hard with the paddle.

*****

April 12, 1962 - I climbed up in the cherry tree to hide today after Mother got so mad about my torn dress. She said I was a brat and a misery to her. I know I am bad.

*****

June 30, 1962 – My nose hurts so much. It's hard to breathe. Mother hit me with her fist.

*****

July 22, 1962 - Mother made me stay inside and stitch today but I stuck my finger and it bled on the quilt. She hit my hands with the metal ruler, and I had to use almost a whole box of Band-Aids. I told Janice and you, diary, but nobody else.

Martha and Lavender exchanged horrified glances. This was their mother's childhood. No wonder she never spoke of it.

"That had to be what happened to the quilt square with the needle still stuck in it, and the rusty stains," Lavender said. "Those were bloodstains. Poor Mom."

They read on, the handwriting growing more mature, and the entries less frequent as Grace grew up. Rhapsodies about her youthful crush on Tommy McGuire in middle school made them smile, until they read of the resulting beating administered by their grandmother.

"I'm glad, now, we didn't know her," Martha said.

June 5, 1970 - Mom got her hands on the insurance money Dad left me. I'm not going to college after all. Mother won again. I hate her, hate, hate, hate her. She'd love to know that. She'd laugh if she read this.

*****

November 1, 1972 - I'll tell Tommy about the baby as soon as he gets home for Thanksgiving break. I hope he'll be as excited as I am. Now if I can only keep Mother from finding out. Janice thinks I'm not safe here, but I don't have anywhere else to go. I'll just have to be extra careful.

*****

November 20, 1972 – I think Mother has guessed I'm pregnant. She twisted the head off my old doll, Susie, and threw it into the fire tonight. It was her crazy way of letting me know she'll kill my baby if she gets a chance.

What am I going to do?

*****

November 21, 1972 - Mother is dead. It was actually easy. When I brewed her herbal tea, I added monkshood. She pinched her nose shut and drank it down, like she always did. Then dying took her most of the night. I'll always hear the sounds. Am I a monster now? What I did was unforgiveable, but I couldn't see another way out. I had to protect my baby.

*****

It was the last entry. Martha and Lavender closed the diary. They didn't meet each other's eyes. Silent tears tracked down Lavender's face. Martha's mouth was set in a grim line.

"Do you remember that strange note you found among her papers?" Martha asked. "Something about monkshood and how she had to do it? Our Mom poisoned her own mother."

"It was because she was scared for her baby," Lavender said. "That must have been why she always grew monkshood. It was punishment to see it growing in her yard every summer, a constant reminder."

"Her worst punishment was keeping that terrible secret," Martha said. "It had to have burned her soul. Do you suppose Dad knew?"

"Who knows? He worshipped her, whether he knew or not."

They sat in silence for a few minutes, wrapped in thought.

"I guess no children ever totally know their parents," Martha finally said. "But this is so far removed from the person I thought I knew, it's hard to wrap my head around it.

Our sweet, gentle mother poisoned our grandmother, who was a dangerous lunatic. How can we ever understand that?"

"Mom was an abused child," Lavender said. "Every day, I work with people escaping from abusive relationships. I see how that experience changes them, what it does to their minds. It seems apparent to us that Mom could have just left, gone somewhere – anywhere – and asked for help. But she was damaged. She couldn't think straight. She'd taken the abuse all her life, but when it came to her baby, something within her drew the line, and she did what she felt she had to do. Then she carried a burden of secrecy all her life. Let's keep faith with her now by never revealing her secret."

"I'll never forget," Martha said, "that *I* was that baby Mom protected. I've wondered, even discussed with Leah, my feeling that Mom never loved me the way she did you. Her concern always seemed to be for you first."

"I blighted your life. I was the problem child, and you always had to take care of me," Lavender said sadly.

"Nonsense," Martha said. "I blighted *yours*, by enabling you to be irresponsible. But we're past that now. We've learned to be better and stronger. No one but you and me will ever know about this, but it means everything to me that Mom loved me so much before I was even born, she killed to protect me."

"What about the diary. Do you want to keep it?"

"No. Do you?"

"No, I'd be afraid someone else would find it someday."

Lavender and Martha walked together to the backyard, to the bare patch where the monkshood had grown. Laying the little book ceremoniously on the ground, Martha flicked the butane lighter she'd grabbed from the kitchen drawer. Flames licked upward as the dry old pages ignited.

In a moment, there was only a wisp of smoke.

The End

ABOUT THE AUTHOR

Doris Reidy's first novel, ***Five for the Money***, was nominated for the 2016 Georgia Author of the Year/First Novel award. ***Every Last Stitch*** is her second book. She lives and

writes in Marietta, Georgia, where she's supported, sustained and entertained by her wonderful children, brilliant friends and vibrant writers' group.

You're invited to visit Doris' webpage, **www.dorisreidy.com**, to follow her blog, read about her writing life and connect with her author pages. Be among the first to hear about her new books by sending your e-mail address to **reidybooks@gmail.com**.

Made in the USA
Lexington, KY
14 May 2017